NeeNee's Accident... Junior Year

Thump. Thump.

I never saw the car coming.

Thump. Thump.

I promise you I didn't.

Thump. Thump.

One minute, my mind was racing with things I wanted to say to Shawn, and then, the next...

Blinding headlights.

Thump. Thump.

Screeching tires.

Thump. Thump.

Somebody was driving like they were drunk.

Thump. Thump.

And then—impact.

Thump. Thump.

And then, the sound of a car speeding away.

They didn't even stop to see if they killed me.

Thump. Thump.

If I was dead.

Thump. Thump.

I thought I was hearing the sounds of some drums, but that was the sound of my heartbeat and the pain that rocked my body.

Thump. Thump.

Pain that had exploded through me as I was thrown into the air.

I was weightless for a terrifying second before crashing down hard to the ground, like a human rag doll would.

The world tilted, the sky spinning above me as shouts and screams filled the air.

My ears rang, and my body refused to move; the sharp, metallic taste of blood filled my mouth. It was my blood.

I gasped for breath and I was forced to swallow more.

My hands instinctively went to my stomach.

Wait! My baby!

Was it too late to protect it?

No!

Through the chaos, I heard Shawn's voice.

Panicked.

Broken.

Scared.

Footsteps pounded against the pavement as others gathered around me, and then, he slid to his knees, beside me.

"NeeNee, stay with me, okay?

His hands hovered over me, shaking.

"Somebody call an ambulance," he yelled.

I tried to speak, but the pain stole my words.

Tears blurred my vision as my hands gripped his.

At least he is here.

Please, God!

Could you not take this away from me, too!

Shawn cupped my face, his own eyes wet with tears.

"Stay with me, baby, please!"

Darkness crept at the edges of my vision, but I fought against it, trying to focus on his face.

I tried to focus on the life growing inside of me.

I heard Shawn scream, "She is pregnant!"

3

Thump. Thump.

I let out a scream.

Thump. Thump.

And then, everything went black…

From the bestselling author
Rasheed Clark

Of the explosive debut novel, *Stories I Wouldn't Tell Nobody But God…*

And the shocking sequel, *Cold Summer Afternoon*, comes…

You Made A Fool Of Me

March Third Imprints

A March Third Imprints Project

Copyright © 2025 by Rasheed Clark

Printed in the United States

ISBN-13: 978-0-9799302-8-7

ISBN-13: 0-9799302-8-6

To My Loyal Readers…

Most people will skip this part, but you should sit down and try to read it anyway. This book is a love letter to you, my loyal readers. It's my way of saying thank you for entrusting me with your time and support.

I know many people are going to look for their names on these pages. If I listed everyone, I will be here all day, and some would be offended, if they were left out. Look at how people act when they are left out of an obituary. So, I chose to say "thank you" to everyone.

I want to thank my loyal readers, not fans, in the past and future. People will say, for years, "I got to read your books," and they never do. They are just talking to be talking. They had how many years? You read it.

Other people will still want a shout-out but didn't do anything to earn it, like in the story of the little red hen who wants to bake some bread. No one would help her. They want the accolades, to be part of something bigger than themselves, but not the responsibility of the consistency for the support that comes with it.

Some would have been mentioned, but never read the book, but will tell people they were mentioned. So and so dedicated this to "me," as if they wrote it.

And above all, I want to thank God.

The one who made me possible, to begin with. People will even say you should have thanked God first. I thank God every day! Why wait for a book to do it? Or even any given Sunday? The most powerful prayer is in saying "thank you" and to practice gratitude daily.

Again, people will always try to tell you what you should have said and what they would have done to control you. I was raised by Elizabeth Louise Clark, an outstanding and phenomenal woman. I am good.

I thank my Mom for finding my writings as a young man and encouraging me to speak the truth. Why lie when the truth will do? To my sister, Jai, thank you! She told me she wouldn't read my first book until I finished it.

My publishing company is called March Third Imprints for a reason. It's her birthday and the day she said it!

And to my oldest son, Javaun, who gave me the idea for this book's title, based on Meshell Ndegeocello's song "Fool of Me." He has been a significant force in this book since the beginning. I needed that support.

When I needed somebody to give me their honest opinion, I talked to him about it, let him read parts, and he said what I needed to hear, in some fantastic conversations, to finish it. This is that book.

Another true story: When he was younger, I remember him walking into my room with my first two books. He knew about the third one. His question? When did I have time to write a book because I was busy raising them? I was also in graduate school again at the time.

I also dedicate this to my loved ones, who once blessed me with their story. I will mention them by name because they are no longer with us. Like my mother, they are my reasons to keep my head held high so they can see who they helped me to become through their presence and they believed in me when others didn't.

8

My brother, Sherman Lamont Clark. My grandmother, Elnora Dunbar Felder. My grandfather, Robert Luckey. My godmother, the marvelous Mrs. Gertrude Pressley Coursey. My uncle, who I called my "Pop," Lawrence "Lonnie" Dunbar. My uncle, Anthony "Ampie" Dunbar.

My aunt, Elisa Felder. The Ms. Thelma Brown, one of my protectors. The phenomenal Ms. Mary Davis. My best friend, growing up, Brian Thomas, who I made a promise to never forget about him. As you can see, I haven't. I named Brian, in my other books, after him.

I'd also like to dedicate this book to the first girl I ever loved. Her name was Yolanda. It started when she would knock on my grandmother's door for things like a pencil or pen. My grandmother eventually said, "He's not home." My grandmother finally told me to talk to her "future granddaughter-in-law." Then, I met her.

I was in love, and she set the basis for how Shawn feels about NeeNee in this book. Sadly, my time with her was cut short when we lost her. She was killed nine days before my birthday; I guess this book is my way of imagining, minus the drama, and all of this book's twists and turns, the happy ending that we never had.

And the last time I saw her, I asked her a question, and she ran off before she would answer it.

And now, why did it take so long to write this...

When I put pen to paper back in 2005, the result was my book, "Stories I Wouldn't Tell Nobody But God." Some people said everything under the sun from how

I "tried" to piggyback off of Terry McMillan's "Waiting To Exhale" when imitation is the highest form of flattery.

Or, I was trying to write the great "American" novel... No, in truth, I set out to write a book that I would want to read. A good book that'll make me want to read it. It's part of why I don't listen to negativity or drama.

With all due respect, I wrote a book that has been selling since 2005 through the power of word of mouth. Without the support of Tyler Perry, or Oprah Winfrey, who people said I should "send" my book to back then, it wasn't meant to be perfect, and neither is this book.

I will tell people it took me six years because I started writing it as a short story in 1998, but didn't finish it. When I found it again in 2005, I went all in. Then, somebody challenged me, asking if I could do it again.

When my girlfriend asked me what I was doing one day, I said nothing. Ten days later, the result of that "nothing" was "Cold Summer Afternoon." With this book, I even deleted the first draft. It wasn't the story I wanted to tell. Then, I had a great conversation with my oldest. Two days later, I had this book. That's all it took.

Just two days—to write this. That's how I move.

I learned that when you know the story you want to tell, and with this book, at least one of the characters, the story will write itself. Since my first two books, I have learned how to deal with the people that some call their "fans" or "followers." I call them my loyal readers.

When I made the jump to Facebook, after having 13,000 connections on Myspace, I learned mental illness is real and it doesn't manifest in people acting crazy, or talking to themselves in public, as we think.

Some people will obsess over you. Now I know why many people call artists their "kings" and "queens"— never themselves. I had one girl "adding" everybody I knew on my page and conversing with them about me.

One asked me if I could sign her book, and then she changed it to "bring" her a copy "personally."

True story. There are so many more stories like it.

And then, there were the "writers," like a couple from Philly, who acted like when I asked them about the publishing business, you'd think I was asking to borrow money, how disrespectful they were. It's not that deep.

I soon learned writers write, authors sell books.

Then, people like Author Eric Jerome Dickey taught me human decency daily and was a light in the dark when I needed guidance. He was given my respect.

My first book was a nod to the movie "The Color Purple," with the title derived from one of the opening lines. I named the main character "Sista." As a kid, I read the book. It was the first movie that I had seen with my mother in the theater. It's my favorite film.

I loved the musical, and sadly, despised the film version of it, outside of Danielle Brooks. "I'm Here" from the musical is one of my favorites. And I when I say despised. I mean despise, not hate. Hate gives people the impression, that I might change my mind.

Then, it came out on Christmas, as if it was a gift.

I wanted my book to be as raw, gritty, and honest as Terry McMillan made "Waiting To Exhale," and when I decided to write it, I wanted to tell the truth. They say if somebody didn't want you to know what they did, then, they shouldn't do it, or have even done it. So I pulled no punches in the things that I wrote.

Every story in my first two books is based on real people and situations I heard about or knew. I did what I do best and put it all together. My sister, knowing all of the players in the books, said the people were going to "beat my ass." I laughed. Never scared, I sent them all copies of the books. I did. Nobody said a word.

Thinking they were Sherlock Holmes, somebody asked if I was "Brian" in my books. I laughed and said, "Yes, and I went to Drexel University. A lot of the words from Sista were from my sister. Day was based on her best friend, and Nikki is a mesh of people I knew regarding her looks and story. That book was a labor of love.

And since that book and the second, so much has happened. After my brother was killed in 2007, I took "Cold Summer Afternoon" off the market because of the subject matter of the shooting. Then, I was reminded of how proud my brother, Lamont, was about my writing. When you buy that book now, the proceeds are still donated to various charities close to my heart.

I have lost so many people, and writing is my form of therapy, and also, my way to immortalize some people in my books. In my first book, Sista's Dad is based on my grandfather, Robert Luckey. Her Mom, my grandmother, Gertrude Barbara Clark.

Any errors in my first book came from the need to tell the story from a first-person point of view, to make it intimate, as somebody would later say, with conversational and realistic dialogue, a heavier depth emotionally, and to make the reader feel like they are being let in on a secret. This book is no different.

Like the songwriter and my birthday twin, Babyface, I have developed enough insight to step into another person's mindset and write from that person's perspective. I'll tell you what a woman, or even a baby, might be thinking. I have been an educator long enough to know how to make an impact with my words.

My writing is said to be raw, emotional, and brutally honest. It often dives into the complexities of human relationships, trauma, and the consequences of our past actions with a confessional, diary-like quality.

It has a dark, cynical humor that balances out the emotional weight. Not everyone will love it. Most people don't even like, or love, themselves.

It's not that fluff that most people will write for shock value or because they think it will pop, like the rappers who will send their kids to private schools but send the average kid who believes in their lyrics to an early grave, or a lengthy prison sentence. And for what?

Or have our girls left with no respect for themselves in the name of fun. Fighting and recording it, I watch enough crime shows to know they are gathering evidence for the cops. And for what? Like it is a bad reality show that should have been canceled.

My books are designed to make you think. To make you feel. To make you laugh. To make you cry. In it, I might drop the word "bitch," but not in a disrespectful way, but it's how some females talk to each other.

Next topic.

I have how many sisters, aunts, and cousins. And if you don't get it, it is not meant to be for you.

I wanted you to hear the characters' voices, making each part personal, engaging, and unfiltered, like the characters are talking directly to you themselves. A book I would not mind reading. We need more books like that. Make me laugh, cry, and make me think.

And movies and television shows. Don't get me started on Tyler Perry's stuff. Feel free to tell him that I said we need to talk. I respect his craft, but with some of his work, there were too many missed opportunities.

Me. I use a lot of symbolism, like doors, coming to and leaving the door reflecting change, and transition. I speak on the actual dynamics of a family, only relatable things. My perception is my reality, and critics are often people who cannot do what you have done but want to tell you how to do it anyway. Show me then.

People still say things like, "Well, I would have made her say," just like people tell children what to say to other people. Or how some adults tell a Black child not to "code switch," which is a sign of intelligence and is like speaking a second language.

Stand down. Please and thank you!

The sins of the fathers, and mothers, for that matter, don't always rest on their children's heads. It's often taught. People will speak through their children, telling them things to say to be cute, and get mad when the child repeats things, like curse words and whatnot, on their own, without that parent's permission.

Can anyone tell you what to say or do? Most people only say things they see on social media. Stand down. That's my nice way of saying, "Shut up!"

Most people don't get it. My mother birthed a leader, not a follower, in me. I am Rasheed Clark.

By the way, "well" is one of the most dismissive words in English. It's like a person listening to respond to you, but not necessarily to understand your words.

When some people want to tell another adult what they should have said or done, they are the ones who lack control over their own lives. The "Well, I would have said…" "Well, you should have told them…"

"You better than me…" or they cut you off when you speak or talk over you, like they know you better than you. That's their pain and emotional turmoil speaking.

Someone once told me I shouldn't say I was mad. I had to correct that person and say, "I am mad because my anger is too expensive, or people could dial it up like a phone number when they want to." People always want to live through you, and not for you. That's sad.

Being "mad" means I refuse to give you any power.

15

And don't get me started on the people who hear I write and always claim they have a story for me—a dry life story with no point. Just talking to be talking.

You cannot please everyone. People will only comprehend things at their level. They often repeat what somebody said to them. Some people only do what is popular, using words like "nice," "good," or how they had "fun" or a "ball," followed by a fake laugh.

Just like "hurt people hurt people," as you will see in this book. I call it "learned behavior," where they only repeat what has been said around them or to them.

Like when somebody tries to hurt your feelings with words that hurt them, their misery wants company.

Me, I don't argue. I don't even try to explain some things to some people. As my mother often said, you don't dignify some things with an answer.

For many things, I still don't.

And this right here is my ninth book—not my third. I got tired of people saying you wrote "a book. "I want to write a book." I was teaching eighth grade, and with the internet, my kids at school were not ready for my books. So I often write nonfiction under other names.

One student, Jihad, went home in 2009 and told his mother that he had learned I was an author. She asked my name, and went into her bedroom, and pulled out my first two books. He came in with the books.

I will tell you this now: NeeNee is a very unique character from my first two books. This is her own stand-alone story. You could, but you don't need to read the other two books to know who she is now.

You could read them, to get the back story, but I got you in this one. Somebody will try to spoil it, but it will only sound crazy. Like in my first book, people couldn't hold water and tried to reveal what happened to Nikki, only for me to flip the script and they got it all wrong.

The character of Ebony is named for the president of my personal fan club since I was younger. She is one of the most amazing people on this planet. I love her. She has always made me feel seen in my life. That is probably the only thing she shares with the character is a name. The Ebony, in this book, is buck wild.

And wait, to the phenomenal Shereatha Green, your amazing friendship inspires me every day. You found me at the darkest point in my life and shined a light.

And if you have read my first two books, do not try to blame me because you were up late trying to finish this. Or you missed your stop on the train. Trust me, you will eventually only hear the characters speaking as you read. Your mind isn't playing tricks on you.

I am always curious as to what that voice sounds like. I have found my "voice" as an author, which is how I write—not for me, but for my readers like you. If this is your first book from me, you are in for a hell of a ride.

And yes, Shawn is based on a younger me. The high school me. I needed somebody I knew well to base this character on. Don't fall in love with him now. Somebody called him messy in the early reads. I loved it. I do!

In the first version, he and Michael, a character you will meet, were brothers and that's why they share similar backgrounds. But he is everything Michael is not. I had to show restraint with this character in a way I have never done. I wrote the book and knew what happens.

Shawn is about as close to me you can get in life, without me writing my life story. Shawn Conquest. Sheed Clark. I normally tell people I am a Capricorn. As in Sheed Clark Capricorn, in homage to my brother, Lamont, who was one, when I wanted to raise hell.

Shawn reflects the best parts of me. Minus, the drama. I hate drama, unless it comes in the form of a book, movie or TV show. That's why if people skip this, they will never know. This is the good part of the book.

The last name Conquest is a real family last name. It the name of the woman who sired part of my lineage. The Euphemia Conquest of Accomack County, Virginia. The name fit the character as you shall see.

We good? We clear? You got all of that.

Glad to hear that! I got tired of explain this.

Hopefully it clears up a lot of things, on the record for a lot of people, who had questions. And for my "critics," why read it just to say you don't like it. Stand down. I put stuff in here that will annoy the literary snobs, like Sapphire did when she wrote the book, "Push." And watch for what Ebony says about "traditions" in this.

And now enjoy the story I have been waiting twenty years to tell. And yes, you'll want to read it again. I did!

NeeNee… Present Day

"Where were you? I called you all weekend!" I asked.

I stood in the middle of Michael's apartment, arms crossed, staring at the man I had spent how many years of my life with, wondering if I had been a damn fool the entire time. I allowed him to, at that.

Michael, never Mike, Michael Johnson, was pacing, looking anywhere but directly at me. He always did that shit. As if Michael is trying to figure out how to deal with me and the situation. He is like that. I am not.

He is six feet three, every bit of 220 hundred pounds, always a well-kept beard and haircut that looks like his barber is a magician. Never a hair out of place.

"I told you, it's complicated." He finally said.

I rolled my eyes so hard that I saw my ancestors. They were upset with him, too.

"Then what is it? This shit is starting to feel real side-chick-ish!" Is that a thing? Side-chick-ish?

Was this my "happily ever after?"

My fairytale that just became a nightmare.

I can still remember the lies that I used to read in books and watch in movies, that one day, a prince, my knight in shining armor, would come to save me.

This was supposed to be him?

He'd ride up on this white horse, as Anita Baker said in her song, "Fairytales," that my Mom used to play in the car with me. Defeat some evil prince to save me.

I believed that part because I couldn't understand everything she said back then. It made everything better. They lied. My prince never showed up.

They sent this motherfucker.

Or maybe they only came for the white ones.

Even in the Disney movies, the only Black Disney princess, Tiana, had a job. Tiana had to save herself and still worked for a living.

"NeeNee," Michael's jaw tightened, and his nostrils flared, his tell-tale sign that he was about to flip this whole conversation on me. "You always do this. You take shit and run with it, instead of trusting me."

There is that word. Run. I should have run by now. If there is one thing that I knew how to do, it was to "run."

Run to shit, run from shit. Run, bitch, run.

Right now, I wanted to run. I should have been a track star. I would have been "that girl," too.

I ran from the pain of my past, from the ghosts that haunted me. I ran from Philly to Washington, D.C., from college to here. I ran from Shawn when I shouldn't have. Who is Shawn, you ask? We'll get to that.

Back to the matter at hand. This one. Michael. Again, never Mike. So formal. So I started again. "How the hell am I going to trust you when you treat the truth like an option. You lie to me like a rug. Is it that deep?"

Silence.

It's always silence with him. When I met Michael, I thought I could stop running from everything. I should have known better.

I should have known this last time when he didn't answer his phone during one of his "family trips" back home, to see his mother, for the weekend. He just disappeared on me. It wasn't the first time either.

It was as if my number popped up on his phone, he would have to explain it to somebody. So I started to think, he just turned his phone off around them.

The kind of shit men do if they go on a "guys" trip," when he was really with some chick in a hotel in Miami.

After a few drinks and an overpriced dinner, that she acts like she is too good to eat, he is in a hotel room, giving her the same three positions he could have given her back home, and she feels special. Dummy.

It was the same excuse when Michael came home this time. It's always something, just like every other time.

"Baby, you know I got a lot going on!"

"It isn't even like that!"

His favorite line is "Why are you bringing up old stuff," about things that happened yesterday.

Tonight, I wasn't about to let that shit go, not when he sat there with the casual arrogance that came naturally to men like him, born into privilege. Men who never had to question their worth. I had questions.

When Michael lied, he let his tongue run over his bottom lip; his gaze would lock on mine like he was trying to figure out how much truth to give me like a man would do a dollar with a fat stripper. His "tell." What was he hiding? I'm curious. Better yet, who?

"Different? Negro, how? Do they bite? Do they speak in tongues? Are they part of some secret society that sacrifices girls like me to the ancestors?" My voice cut through the stillness of the apartment, and my tone was laced with frustration. He had to hear it.

Yet, here we were again. My arms were crossed, face twisted, while Michael, stood there running that same tired script. He reused things more than Tyler Perry.

How many Tyler Perry movies have you watched where you kept asking, "Where have I seen this before?" Even now, I have been here before with Michael. The only difference is that I am tired now.

The person you choose to be with affects everything in your life. Your mental health. The love inside of you. Your happiness. How you get through tragedies. Your success. How your children will be raised? Who you will eventually become. Everything. Choose wisely.

At that moment, I caught a glimpse of myself in the mirror. With those dark brown eyes that never quite could hide my past hurts or pain, I looked hard at myself. At only five feet six inches, with a chocolate complexion, slim, and straight, long hair, I deserved more than arguing with him about this again.

He couldn't even look at me. My looks usually made men stare, but I don't think I ever carried myself like I believed in why. I closed my eyes, took a deep breath, and looked at Michael again. He didn't look back.

"So let me get this straight," I said with my voice low, but tight. "We've been together for how long, but somehow I haven't been good enough to meet your family? And then, there's all of this secrecy with you?"

Michael sighed, rubbing his temple likes I was giving him a damn headache. "NeeNee, it's not even like that." There it is. I was finally getting to him.

"Then talk to me?" I said. My arms were crossed so tight against my chest, as if I was holding myself together. "What is it? Where were you?"

Michael's jaw flexed, as he kept rubbing his hands, as if he was trying to control himself, like he tries to control me at times with his lies. I allowed him to do it though.

His head snapped up. "Are you fucking serious right now? What is next? That I have a wife too?"

I laughed. "I don't know, Michael. Do you? I could be your backup plan." Yes, I said it. I know that sounded dumb. I was saying anything at that point. People do stuff like that. Don't judge me.

Michael walked towards where I was, his jaw clenched and towering above me. He was upset with me.

He was looking at me, but he was the one standing there with secrets in his eyes and a bunch of half-truths on his lips, and for the first time, after praying to God that I would meet somebody different, I saw that he wasn't that. He reminded me of my father.

Now here I wanted to finally break that stereotype, that girls really do date men like their fathers, and guys date women like their mothers. Let's keep it real. Many do.

Maybe that's why when women get into relationships, they start to act like that man's mother, and men act like children and need to be taken care of. Ebony and her psychology stuff had gotten to me over the years.

I realized my prayers had gone unanswered. And that hurt more than anything. And if God didn't have any more jokes, softly in the background, Meshell Ndegeocello's "Fool of Me" was playing on the radio. I used to love that song before Michael. I really did.

And just then, it got to that one part of the song that I don't sing, at least not anymore, where she says "I feel so dumb…" I looked at Michael again, and I did.

I felt dumb. Stupid. And in that moment, I knew why I would rather be single, and know what I want, than to be in a relationship like this, and not get what I needed.

If love was in the air, I would be holding my breath…

A Stranger In My House…

Michael glared at me. "Do you think I would be here every night if I had a wife somewhere?"

He could have a side chick though. Or was I her?

"Men do it all the time," I shot back refusing to back down. "And if you aren't married, what is the excuse? If you are cheating on me, at least have some decency to tell me. When was the last time you fucked me?"

He hesitated. I had struck a nerve. Good.

Michael's frustration filled the space between us. It was the kind of frustration that only came when a man felt like he was talking to a brick wall. This was that.

"Oh," I laughed. "Now you are quiet again."

I leaned back against the kitchen counter, giving him a once-over, trying to provoke him.

People tend to tell the truth when they are angry. Maybe, he'd blurt out the truth. Get emotional.

My problem also was that he was distracting me. He always looked good. Too damn good.

His skin almost glowed under the dim lights.

He had an almost intimidating confidence, and he wore it like a suit of armor. Like his Penn law school T-shirt, his arrogance was stretched across his chest.

He chose that school. His other alma matter.

Yes, he is smart. And yet, he is the kind of man who made you feel stupid, and could still play dumb himself a lot. He was doing it now. That was his thing.

How could he be this great lawyer and not know how to argue? Me, I sounded like my mother did with my father. I still remembered that and hated myself for it.

"You go home all the time. I could see if you were going to the moon. Your parents live on Long Island. We are in the city. Give me their address. I will go introduce myself. Let them know, hey, I got you."

I know it sounded stupid the minute that I said it. I hated when he pushed me into corners, and I had to feel like I had to prove myself. Is this what my mother felt like?

He ran a hand down his face. "I just don't bring women home like that. Not just anybody. My mother doesn't do 'outsiders.' My family is… complicated."

If this son of a bitch says that word one more time… I will beat his ass. I was already tired of this dance.

Then, it hit me… maybe, I wasn't good enough.

It tugged at me all the time. I felt it now.

My father gutted my family when he traded his wedding vows for his other woman's bed and that's how I lost my mother to all of that.

I wanted to be a part of a family, even if it wasn't my own. Maybe I was fooling myself, even now.

And that thought, just one thought, that ugly, familiar thought, took me right back to my childhood.

I had never been "enough." For my mother, with her ever-growing vacant eyes and cold words.

For my father, given how he left us.

For the light-skinned complexion girl, who said I was "pretty," even though my skin is "dark."

For every white person who saw my dark skin, and thought I was about to be ghetto, or some angry Black woman, before I said a word.

For every man I had met, since my father, always trying to prove I was worthy of love.

I forced a laugh, shaking my head. So I said what I was thinking out loud.

"You know… they say girls date men like their fathers. That's probably why they are so quick to call that man 'daddy.' Waiting for the day he disappoints her, like her father did. My father kept secrets too. I prayed you'd be different. That you'd be better. I was wrong."

That hit him. I didn't care. I wanted him to hurt.

Just like he made me feel in all of this.

His expression hardened, his fists clenched at his side, but I wasn't afraid of him hitting me.

"Don't do that." He glared at me as if he knew something that I didn't. Something funny. He didn't laugh though. "I am trying to be better for you."

Hurt people hurt people. That hurt him. But why?

"Don't do what? Speak the truth? And how?" I asked.

I crossed my arms again, and stared at him like he was a stranger. Reminding him that he was the issue right now, not me. I just wanted to know where he went.

Maybe that was my abandonment issues talking.

Maybe I had spent all this time trying to build something with someone who never saw me as permanent.

Maybe, I filled a space, a now, and not a forever.

Maybe this was all for show on his part. If this was Shawn, I would have run by now, but I was trying to be different. I was trying to do things differently.

Michael walked out of the room, but, this conversation wasn't over by a long shot.

I looked at the time. It was too late to call Ebony, but I would in the morning. She had to hear about this one. She was the only one who would understand...

Girl…

"So what are you going to do? Sit there and stress, or are you going to do something?" Ebony asked.

I was sitting at my desk at work, and Ebony Mitchell, everyone calls her "B or Eb," my best friend in the world, and my ride-or-die sister, was on the phone.

She didn't even let me finish venting before she started plotting. Ebony is usually my voice of reason.

Not today.

"I am not stressing," I replied. I lied.

"Girl, I can picture you sitting there looking out the window like a sad Mary J. Blige or Keyshia Cole song. Oh, let me not say a name like Keisha around you."

It made me turn around, as if, she could see me.

I ignored that last part about Keisha.

"It is starting to bother me why I never met his family?" I replied. "And he didn't call me all weekend. He's up to something. I just don't know what it is? Or is it me?"

Ebony took a deep breath, and then, she said what I needed to hear… "It is not you. But did you forget who I am? We have other ways of figuring this shit out."

I was almost too scared to ask, but I did. "How?"

"We need to pop up at his job with two pieces of chicken and a biscuit. Scope shit out. See if anything is going on there lately Have you been to his new job?"

Michael had been named partner months ago at a new firm. He said that is why he was working so hard.

I blinked. "Bitch, what? Lord, we are going to jail. No."

And pop up? I could already picture it. Ebony will pretend to not speak English, and I'll be hard of hearing, as we sit in the back of the squad car.

Ebony was about that life. She is from Brooklyn.

"You heard me. He wants to be all 'it's complicated.' Let's make it very simple. We pull up since he said he is always working "late," and see if he is even there. You bring him dinner, and we see how he reacts."

I hesitated. "That feels like... I don't know... crazy crazy? I am from Philly, but damn. I'm good."

She laughed in my ear. "Girl, you are dating a man who won't even claim you to his mother. Crazy already left the chat. Pull up to his job. Surprise him with food; if he isn't acting funny, he will be happy to see you."

I sighed, "I just don't want to be 'that girl,' B."

"That girl?" I could feel her irritation growing. "The girl who expects bare minimum respect? The girl who doesn't want to be a secret? He is lying, sneaking around. Disappearing. Chile, if that is 'that girl,' then you need to be her ASAP. Sis, you are already her! You might as well commit to it. Main character energy."

She had a point. Ebony always had a point.

That's how I found myself outside of Michael's office a few hours later, holding a tray of oxtails and rice from his favorite Jamaican spot, like I was the perfect girlfriend, with a lot of anxiety.

He said he would be working late. Surprise!

Only I didn't get the perfect reaction.

The receptionist gave me a confused look when Michael wasn't answering his phone. She tried again. Now at that point, I was confused.

"Do you know if he has left for the day?"

Before she could answer, a voice cut in.

I turned around, and I won't lie, she was stunning in that intimidating, high-maintenance way.

Tall, caramel-skinned with sleek shoulder-length hair that was too perfect for her to be anything less than high-maintenance. Her suit hugged every curve, her makeup flawless at this hour, and her energy?

Unbearable.

I have been here before. I knew her type. Extra. Over the top. The minute she walked up to me, she looked me up and down. I was dressed in a simple top, jacket, and pants—nothing special.

"Can I help you?" She asked.

I smiled, trying to keep it friendly, and cordial.

"I am here to see, Michael Johnson."

Her lips curled into something that wasn't quite a smirk. "Oh, you must be Nay Nay."

Strike one. She went there. That name reminds me too much of my mother's. She got my name wrong on purpose. As a Black female, my name is my identity.

Say it right!

"NeeNee," I corrected her.

I frowned, "And you are?"

She leaned against the desk, eyes gleaming with amusement. She knew that I knew who she was.

She said, stressing every syllable, "My name is Monica. Michael and I work closely together. You must be the girlfriend. Cute."

Cute? What does that mean?

I don't know why, but something about how she said "work closely together," made my stomach sour. If she had not already fucked Michael, she looked like it was on her to-do list. Was she the issue?

"He's not here," she continued. "But I can let him know you stopped by. If he wanted you to know his schedule, I assume he would have told you. He said he had dinner plans, and I guess you weren't invited. Shame too. He has such great taste in restaurants, and food."

She looked at the tray of food. Such audacity.

I forced a tight smile. "That won't be necessary. I will call him later."

"You do that," she said sweetly, before she turned to walk away. "Cheer up. I am sure he will make it up to you. Or you can eat that. It smells interesting."

I walked out feeling unsettled, realizing something was off. And Ebony, she was livid when I told her.

"Oh, hell no." Ebony was pacing when I got back to our place. "Oh, no, she didn't."

I sighed, "It's probably nothing."

"Girl, nothing? You just met his new bitch-in-training. She just told you to stay in your lane, and you went and parked. Do you even hear yourself?"

I knew about Monica. She wasn't "new." She was Michael's "colleague." He mentioned her before, when he became a partner at this new firm.

Did he send her out to run interference?

I thought back to all the casual ways Michael said Monica this, and Monica that, in the last couple of months. I knew her type all too well.

She reminded me of that Keisha. Never mind.

I called Michael again. Not once, but twice.

Straight to voicemail.

I hated that my gut was telling me the same thing Ebony said. Michael was hiding something.

Was it Monica though?

When I first arrived, I didn't want to tell Ebony what I had seen outside his office.

Michael's silver Aston Martin was still there with a license plate that said "Michael J."

I touched the hood, and the engine was cold, like it had not moved all day.

Make Him Do Right...

"So where the fuck did you go?" I asked later that night. I had repeatedly asked the same question for the last ten minutes. I didn't want to bring Monica up.

It was like we were having the same conversation.

He keeps lying to me.

What is with all of the secrecy?

If he was sleeping with somebody else, anybody else, the only thing that I didn't want him to do was "play" in my face about this, and disappearing last weekend, without a word. I just wanted the truth.

Standing here now, he looked like he didn't give a damn about anything that I had to say. I had allowed him, in my own way, to make me feel like this.

He was hiding something. But what?

"Fine," I said. "I give up."

Michael was still staring at me like I was crazy.

Like I was "complicated." You hear a word enough; you eventually start using it. He used to make me feel like I am something special and worth the effort.

Late-night conversations that turned into morning coffee runs. My bed felt less lonely when he was in it. He was always the perfect gentleman.

I needed that Michael again.

I even settled for the mediocre sex that we had, even if we only did it once a month, where he penciled me into his schedule. And only with a condom, despite our tests, to keep me from getting pregnant. Or getting any of his money until we were married, I guess.

Sometimes I wondered if I was enough because he always wanted to "try things." Experiment.

Is that what this is about?

Me not giving into that Scorpio freak shit? Maybe.

For a while, I let myself believe that he was different. I should have run away. I still could.

I am standing in Michael's apartment, watching him shut me out again.

Michael looked at me, searching my face for an idea, or a clue, about what I was about to say.

I saw that look again. Was he enjoying this?

He moved closer to me.

"The night we met, you looked at me like I was different. You trusted me." He said quietly.

I let out a breath. "I thought you were. I wanted you to be. I wanted us to be different."

The air grew thick and heavy with everything we weren't saying.

But it wasn't enough. I wasn't enough.

"You know what," I finally said defeated. My voice was barely a whisper. "Keep your damn secrets. I am even done begging for a seat at your family's table that I wasn't invited to. I will give you back your keys."

"NeeNee, wait—" For once he looked scared.

Good. Finally. Something other than his usual bullshit.

"What is it, Michael? What is it now?" I could take anything, but his silence. I stepped closer, my voice stronger, so each word cut like a knife.

"I have been your girlfriend. You even said that you wanted to marry me. I have slept in your bed, cooked your food, held you down, and you still ain't introduce me to the people that made you, or raised you? Then, there is all of this secrecy. I am tired, Michael."

"NeeNee, stop! You don't know what you are talking about." Did I see something else in his eyes?

Like he wanted to tell me the truth? Finally!

"No, you stop! I don't know shit because you don't tell me shit!" I shot back. My anger was building.

"You act like I am a random chick off the street. Why do I always feel like a secret if I'm so important to you?"

I finally said it.

The result… silence.

There it was again. It was real and not a dream or fantasy. It stretched between us, thick and suffocating.

Michael wasn't used to being questioned.

He liked control, and I was finally realizing that. Just then, his eyes softened, and for a brief second, I saw the person I had been introduced to.

"NeeNee, just trust me." He finally said.

Trust him? Not when he pretended to take me to the next level, but I felt like I was dragging him there.

That is my answer. I had spent years learning to read people and sense the weight of their unspoken judgment and words. There's more to this story.

If there was one thing I realized about Michael at that moment, it was that he was not about to tell me the truth. He would lie first. I am grown now. I can take it.

I should have left right then and there, but I didn't. That is what women, like me, do. We stay.

We stay too long, hoping men, like him, will turn into something that they ain't. He is just like my father.

And I promised myself and God that I wouldn't be like my mother. She was stupid for that. I already lived with the mistakes that she made my entire life.

Eventually children get old enough to see which parent was the issue. For me, it was the both of them.

I was ready to walk away from Michael. Run, actually.

And just then, he did the one thing I didn't expect.

He walked away. He sure did.

I figured oh, well, given that some people will lie on their Mama, and to God, if they think it will help them.

I was tired of being understanding. It made me overlook his disrespect.

I thought he was about to go in the bedroom and basically say the hell with me for the rest of the night.

Instead, he did something that surprised me.

He walked over to his bag, opened it, and pulled out a ring box—that kind of box.

He looked at me and said, "I wanted to wait until you met my mother, but I am tired of waiting. You deserve this moment. I went out to buy this earlier—the ring you saw. This is why I wasn't at the office. I went to get this."

He got down on one knee in another Penn shirt, and asked, "Will you marry me…"

They Don't Know About Us...

The restaurant was five-starred. Fancy. It was a place where men in tailored suits ordered overpriced steaks, and women sipped wine, like it was a social sport.

It was quiet.

Very quiet.

Too quiet.

It was like a library, or a funeral. I hated the quiet.

It is the kind of place Michael would walk into and be greeted with familiarity and seated, but other people would need months of begging just to get a reservation.

Shawn would have used his charm to get in here with no reservation. Was that it? I was subconsciously comparing Michael to Shawn. It struck me like a bell that Michael was everything that Shawn wasn't.

And this place. It was the kind of place that he liked, even if tonight was supposed to be a celebration, because Michael had closed a deal with a new client.

I looked around again. I had been here far too many times to count. I realized it wasn't about the food but the quiet for Michael. He paid for the silence.

Money brings quiet. Have you ever noticed that the most expensive places, like a bank or country club, are quiet? Target is quiet.

It was a place where people knew how to act, talk, and carry themselves in a certain way. Where you didn't have to worry about being seen.

It would protect whatever secret you had. You could bring your mistress here, and they would treat her the same as your wife. And she probably wouldn't notice any of it. She was just happy to be seen and outside.

"They didn't let the "riff-raff" in," Michael said when we first came here. "The loud chicks, and their drug dealer boyfriends, with his pants hanging off their asses."

I wanted to ask, "Ghetto shit? Or people like me?"

It is the kind of place where the patrons knew the chef.

There were no brand labels on anyone's clothing.

No Balenciaga shoes. Gucci belts. Or labeled bags.

Michael didn't like labels at all. He didn't even wear sneakers. I couldn't understand that either.

When I first met Michael, he took me shopping. I tried to buy shirts that said Gucci on the front, He made me put it back. That is when I first saw the change in him.

Michael said "that shit" was for "broke-ass people." Not all Black people are broke. He said you can tell when a person is impressed by money when they have to show off a brand. Is this the life he was preparing me for?

He said people should have to tell you what they are wearing, like on the award shows, after you compliment them about it.

That night, I was moving his shirt. The purple label said Ralph Lauren, as in Polo, and I looked at the front of it. It didn't have a jockey and horse logo. He knew.

I looked at Michael, as he was picking through his salad, as he looked at his iPhone. He was trying to carry on a half-assed conversation with me. At least he was trying to talk to me now. It wasn't always like this.

His cologne was subtle. He could have worn a sweat suit, and it would have looked like a tuxedo. Instead, he was still dressed in a stylish black suit from work that fit his frame like it had been made for him recently. It had to be. I don't recall ever seeing it.

He was from this world. Rich. Monied. Classy.

I wasn't. Michael needed all of this.

It was his world. I was just there. I hated it.

I am just NeeNee, the scholarship girl, who lost my mother to herself, and my father, and our family to my mother's "best friend." I was left to fend for myself in a world that never made room for me.

I did my best to manage though.

Like my father's new wife, I never wanted to be a second choice. I wouldn't dare speak her name. She broke my mother, and crushed me.

I knew my stepmother's name, if you can call her that. Stepmother. She never stepped up, or in, for me. My mother called her that "bitch." That's what I call her too.

I adjusted my dress in my seat.

Tonight, after work, I changed into a nicer dress. Even though Ebony ensured I was dressed to fit the occasion and place, I still felt out of place. My hair was up in a tight ponytail. I wore a red dress that turned heads as I walked in. I did this for Michael, not for me.

I looked good, even if I didn't always feel it. Everyone in the restaurant looked at me when I walked in, but Michael, as usual, ignored it. He was used to this.

Maybe I bored him.

As an entertainment lawyer, I guess he was used to the bad "bitches," actresses, singers, models, and his clients, that made New York their home.

The Monicas of the world.

The fact that he had chosen to propose to me, I should have felt lucky. I should be happy. He chose me. I wasn't. We had not had sex since. I didn't press the issue. Neither did he. It was another aspect of my life with him, boring sex after the first time.

I sat across from him, my hands resting on the white linen tablecloth, my engagement ring catching the light. It felt heavy. Lately, everything about this relationship felt heavy. It was almost suffocating lately.

Just then, I realized that Michael was talking still, his deep voice smooth, calculated, almost rehearsed. I caught something about meeting his mother, but his words didn't initially register. I really wasn't listening.

43

I took a sip of my wine slowly, letting it roll over my tongue, trying to process what he said.

After so many years together and being engaged for how many weeks, I should've met her by now, but Michael always had an excuse, even now.

"She's busy."

"She's traveling."

"It's not the right time."

Now, suddenly, it was the right time.

I glanced up at him, taking in his chiseled jawline, smooth brown skin, and eyes that used to make my knees feel weak. Now I just felt tired. He did that.

Something had changed between us, but I couldn't understand what. Maybe he stopped trying because this ring was it, and it meant he had me.

He won. He claimed me.

He had shut me up. I will be quiet now.

"When?" I asked, as our food was served.

"Tomorrow night," he said, cutting into his steak.

He didn't say his prayers before he ate, like God already owed him that meal.

"She wants to have dinner at the house on Long Island in Old Westbury. My mother's been asking."

Now I knew he was lying.

Michael's mother never asked about me.

She had not even acknowledged my existence in the last few weeks. He talked to her every single day.

That's what made this so weird.

She wasn't the type of woman who welcomed outsiders, he made that clear. Broke people. People from a different social scene. I don't know.

And to her, I was an outsider. He had said it.

I set my glass down. "So, she just magically decided she wants to meet me now?"

Michael sighed like I was exhausting him, like I was the one being difficult now.

Again. Still. I do not fucking know.

"NeeNee, come on. She's important to me. I need for her to like you. She thinks I need to settle down."

Need? So, was this her idea or his to marry me?

Instead, I asked, "Like me, or approve of me?"

His silence was my answer.

I leaned back in my chair. "Michael, are we engaged, or am I just auditioning for the role of an 'acceptable wife'?" Or a trophy for your mother's approval?"

Michael's jaw tightened. "You're making this a bigger deal than it is. She merely said she is happy for us."

"I don't think I am." I toyed with my fork, tracing patterns into the pasta on my plate. "She's never cared to meet me before. Why now? This feels so sudden."

Michael hesitated. "Because I told her I asked you to marry me. And she had... questions."

I laughed, but not because it was funny. "Questions? Like what? I'm confused? About what? Tell me."

He shrugged like it was nothing. "Where you are from? Your background—"

"My background?" My voice had an edge now. "What? Like for a damn job interview?"

"NeeNee!" He was getting angry again.

"No, Michael, tell me. What about my 'background' is so questionable? What did you tell her?"

His silence stretched between us, thick and suffocating. I knew what this was. There it is. I wasn't good enough for him, or his mother.

"I just need you to come, okay?" he said finally, his voice softer now, as if that would smooth over the insult. "Please. You will be the mother of my children."

46

I winced when he said "children" because of... I stopped myself and tried to shake that thought out of my mind. Could I even have another child? Then, he said "children." Plural. That means more than one.

I forgot Michael doesn't know about "that" time in my life, or Shawn. He never asked about my past relationships, and I never told him anything. I never asked about his. We were even, I guess.

I could've said no. I could've walked away right then, tossed the ring on the table, and been done with it.

But I didn't.

Part of me—the stupid, hopeful, still-in-love part— wanted to believe that meeting his mother wasn't a test.

That maybe, just maybe, I wouldn't end up disappointed this time. She will love me.

I exhaled, and nodded. I wasn't going to run this time. I had been running my whole life. Just like my father.

Just like I ran from Shawn.

For a brief instance, I thought about Shawn.

"Fine." I replied, and finished eating.

For a minute, I caught a glimpse of myself in the mirror, just beyond Michael. They put mirrors in places like this, and bars, where people wouldn't like seeing themselves being rude to the staff. I saw my father in my face, and questioned if I was making a mistake.

And then, I stopped and looked again. I saw my mother and said a silent prayer that I wasn't like either of them. I didn't want to be.

Two emotionally unavailable people who made me feel like my needs were too much.

My mother used me to trap my father into marriage though. I looked at Michael, who already had everything, could I even give him even one baby, or "children?"

Michael briefly looked at me.

He stopped eating, as if he was trying to read my mind. I looked away, so he wouldn't be able to.

If he knew about Shawn, what would he say?

What would he do?

Or about my mother, my father?

I looked back at myself in the mirror and for the first time in a long time, I was scared…

Papa Was A Rolling Stone...

I think I was a little girl the last time I saw my father.

I vaguely remember standing in the doorway of my parents' bedroom in our apartment in New York, watching him pack.

He always seemed like a giant to me.

Tall, dark-skinned complexion.

Growing up, I would see pictures of and movies with the actor Morris Chestnut and have to tell myself that that wasn't him.

At that moment, as he packed to leave, I asked him where he was going. That's where my abandonment issues started. It had to be.

He already seemed angry. My parents arguing back then had woken me up out of my sleep.

He looked at me, and then, at my mother, who was curled up on the couch, staring blankly at the TV. It wasn't even on. She was never this quiet.

Her chocolate skin would later match my own, but I didn't want to be anything like her.

My father didn't answer me, he just left.

Did he even say goodbye? Or even try?

He ran. Maybe that's where I got it from.

My mother didn't cry.

She didn't scream.

She just sat there, sinking deeper into whatever darkness had eaten away at her for years. After that, I spent days at my Aunt Shirley's place, my Mom's other best friend, in Philadelphia. Philly Philly. She lived in what they called the "Bottom" of West Philadelphia.

Her house was nasty. She rarely cleaned up.

The next time I would see my mother, she picked me up, we headed back to New York, and she scrambled to pack everything she owned with my Aunt Shirley's help. I never understood why.

"Men ain't shit," I heard my mother say over and over again. "They take and they take and when you are done, they leave you broken."

Some nights when it gets too quiet, I can still remember the nights my Mom cried herself to sleep about my father, after we left New York.

There were other men, too. They came and went, too. I didn't even know their names. I could tell that she was lonely, but she never said it.

After the last one, she barely spoke to me.

She'd shuffle around, and mumbled.

My mother never said my father's name. At least I don't remember her saying it ever again.

And then one day, she left too.

Not physically—her body was still there, at first, but her spirit was gone. She had been broken.

She folded into herself.

She drowned, in her sadness, that eventually took her away from me. I was truly alone.

The only thing she left me with was my name. My nickname. I refused to be called anything else. NeeNee, like Knee Knee. Never Ni---

One day, my Aunt Shirley told me how I got my name, to be smart. And I was furious.

"You know..." she started. My father named me after one of his exes. He was in love with yet another woman, and she left him for somebody else, too.

Typical. Good for her though.

What goes around comes back around.

But that is a story for another time, and a story most people would say I shouldn't tell nobody but God. My parents were a lot. They were toxic.

I soon learned that my father had a whole new life now, including a new wife and another child—so I heard—a brother or sister that I never met.

For a minute, we lived "good" on my mom's money. Then, somehow, that was gone. Maybe one of those guys took it. We were broke after that. Homeless.

When my Mom got tired of running—we had even lived in Mexico for a minute—she dropped me off again at Aunt Shirley's place. I was 13 or 14, when I realized Aunt Shirley didn't even want me there.

I was a burden. I was another mouth to feed, and an extra chore. She never made me feel like I belonged. She was as fake with some people around me, and loud and ghetto with others about it. I hated her for it.

I was the trophy she trotted out when she wanted the attention. She'd say how she took me in, and how I needed her so desperately. To her, I was ungrateful.

She had suddenly found God after years of her bullshit, but I doubt if God knew she was even lost. She was nothing more than sharp edges and disapproving stares at that point. Aunt Shirley was "stiff."

She was built like a mean bulldog. She was so nice when I was younger, when my Mom was around to protect me. How were they even friends?

She was different when I lived with her and her children in her house. I couldn't run away. I didn't have anywhere else to go. I was scared of foster care. I went to school every day to get away from that place.

I always felt like my Mom did something to her, and she never forgave her for it. Did she owe her money, or something? I don't know. It seemed like it.

She told me, "You eat what I cook. You don't touch anything that doesn't belong to you. You stay out of my way! Do you hear me?" That's exactly what I did.

I realized, if that woman had a warm bone in her body, I never saw it. To this day, I hate to hear a car door slam, because of my time at her house.

I could still hear the slam of the car door when my mother dropped me off at Shirley's house. It feels like a lifetime ago. My suitcase rolled behind me for what I thought would be only a couple of days.

She'd come back. She promised. She said she would.

It turned into days, months, and then, years.

She lied. And I learned to lie to myself. Make shit up.

Telling myself whatever I had to get through my days when times got hard. Sometimes, I would imagine my parents were still together and we were all happy.

That's why I didn't have any friends. What would I say when they found out that the things I said weren't true? Nobody even showed up for my report cards or awards.

At my graduation, I remember looking out into the crowd praying my mother would show up. She never came. I stayed until they locked the doors. I did.

I know I am all over the place talking about this, because it still hurts, and you need to know.

Again, Shirley had her children—her precious children. She reminded me I wasn't one of them, so I stayed to myself. They could do no wrong. Not me.

I was an extra mouth to feed, even if she did get a welfare check for me, and then, kinship care money because she lied and told the foster people that I was her "niece." The little girl who looked too much like her daddy for her to even pretend to love, according to her.

She never outright said it, but it was in the little things. I always wondered where my Mom's actual sister, my real aunt, or even my grandmother, who used to keep me, were. Or my father's Mom and Dad?

With Shirley, I saw how she made sure her children had second helpings at dinner, but my plate was cleared when I was done my first plate. I didn't care. Her food was nasty anyway, just like her house. When company came, she'd yell at me for the place not being clean.

She would let her kids have sleepovers, but I couldn't have any company. I had to be in my room with the door closed. So I learned how to disappear. How to make myself small, so I wouldn't take up too much space in a house that wasn't mine.

Always quiet. By myself. I felt alone. I was alone.

And the first chance I got, I left. I ran.

I got into college on a full-ride academic scholarship. I saved up what little money I could working at the market, packed my bags, and never looked back. I never asked Shirley for anything. And I even gave her $50 a week out of my check. Yeah, she was like that.

No, I didn't even invite Aunt Shirley's messy ass to my graduation. What for? That summer, I stayed at school at a college orientation program until classes started.

Failure was not an option because the truth is, I had no where else to go. No home. No family. Just me.

At college, I could be invisible. I could make my own way. And until freshman week, I did, until I met Ebony. My Ebony, my ride or die. My rock. My best friend.

Ebony is only 5'4 with a thick frame with curves that clung to her like sin. Trust me, Ebony was a full-fledged menace. You'd pray when you see her coming. Skin the color of dark honey, a head full of long honey blonde hair that she kept in braids. Her mouth never took a day off. Ebony was more sociable than me.

A crazy Pisces, like me, she really could talk a preacher into throwing ones at a strip club and make you laugh at your worst moment. She was always quoting lines from movies. I used to wonder sometimes if I made Ebony up in my head. But, no, she was very real.

Ebony took a seat next to me at freshman orientation, and said the one thing I needed to hear, "If we become friends, I will fight every dirty bitch up in here for you."

She meant it. Daring anyone to look at me wrong.

I finally had somebody to love me for me and me for her. And I later learned why. She needed somebody too. She was an only child and I didn't know that first day, she wasn't the type to let go of anything easily.

During the holidays, I used my student loan refund checks to stay in a cheap motel until school opened back up. I am from Philly. I did what I had to do to survive back then. I wasn't going to sell my ass, or my soul. Ebony would be back soon enough. I was okay.

When Ebony, found out I spent that Thanksgiving at a motel, she dragged me during that first winter break to stay with her grandmother, Ms. Mary, in Brooklyn. It was in a high-rise apartment. It was tiny, but it felt like home. It was safe and clean. Ebony made sure of that.

During the holidays, it made me happy just to be there. I never stopped thinking about my father though. Sometimes, I would call his number to hear his voice, on his voicemail. I found his number online.

I never left a message. I never dared to say anything. I just hung up, and hated myself for it. I just wanted to remind myself that he was alive. That he could have found me, if he wanted to. He never tried. Outside of Ebony, I didn't trust anyone, for real.

I don't even trust Michael now. I tried to. I did.

Then Shawn showed up—Shawn Shawn, Shawn Jonathan Conquest. If I can't tell you about Shawn, then you would never understand why I feel this way about Michael right now.

I thought that was why you were reading this: to find out why I am who I am, how I got to be here, and why I am so insecure. I am, you know. Still.

This about to be like in the movies, and the main character is in some shit, and you are wondering how they got to be who they are, and what happened.

This is about to be that. I know you want to know what happened to my baby, and if it was Shawn's...

You Don't Know My Name...

So let me tell you about Shawn... that Shawn!

I met Shawn Jonathan Conquest during my sophomore year in college, back when love was something I thought I understood. When I believed somebody's touch could erase loneliness, chemistry was enough to build something lasting. He was a junior.

I had tried to date and had met a couple of people, but I soon realized I didn't know how to date. So, I developed a relationship with my grades. I had seen Shawn around campus, but I was invisible to him in my thrift shop clothes. I was always studying or with Ebony. She knew everybody's name. I didn't.

Then, fate stepped in. God. Whatever.

It was an early Monday morning, the second week of school, and too early for a business law class. The classroom smelled like coffee and regret, filled with students who had either partied too hard the entire weekend or were already counting down to the semester's end. I was neither.

I spent most nights studying because I refused to fail a class that cost more than some people's rent. Didn't I tell you failure was not an option? I had a single dorm room, thank God. I worked on campus. I was on a scholarship. I was broke, but I had plans.

Shawn always walked in, and sat in the row behind me in the back of the room, slouching in his seat like he had all the time in the world. No books. No bag. No pencil, as usual. At least he was on time, as the other people came in. When class started, I ignored him.

Shawn was the kind of man who knew the world worked in his favor, who could talk his way in and out of anything and everything, especially some panties. At least, not mine. That is what I heard from Ebony.

A basketball star. He was team captain. Rich. Spoiled. Tall. His dad was a top executive at a major real estate and construction company in Atlanta.

Player, player for sure. He knew it.

"Too attractive to be single," according to Ebony the first time I saw him on campus last year.

You didn't have to see him to feel his presence. He was why storms had names. He had that kind of confidence that didn't need to be announced, it just was.

He knew it too. He walked like he knew it.

The last time I saw anything like that was in a guy from high school named Rasheed. We called him Clark.

You always saw Rasheed, because his ass never went to class. He was always in trouble. Suspensions were a semi-vacation to him. He was smart too. Could have been class valedictorian. Like he knew his shit. He would learn the rules to break them--and you, if and when he needed to. Don't sleep on that kind of person.

When Rasheed used to walk down the halls, you just knew he knew he wasn't arrogant. He just knew who he was, and didn't need to explain it. You knew when he walked into a room. You wanted to know who he was and when he left, he still left you guessing.

With Shawn, it was that same kind of energy. I've seen him walk through campus. He talked to everybody, but me. Ebony knew him. Okay, she knew of him, I'll say.

So the first time I "met" Shawn, I was flipping through my notes, trying to make sense of legal jargon that might as well been written in Greek.

Professor Davis was droning on about contract law, and I was also fighting to stay awake. I had worked the night before. Then, I heard him, and that voice.

"That man has got to be at least a hundred years old," Shawn muttered behind me. "He probably wrote the first laws himself. Gave Moses a commandment."

I laughed, but I didn't turn around.

"Every time he blinks, I hold my breath because I don't know if he will make it."

I covered my mouth to keep from laughing.

"I will bet you he was a substitute teacher when Jesus was in school." He was so corny.

"He might write in Roman numerals and we'll have to Google our grade." I laughed, and finally turned around, and I was met with that mischievous smile and the weight of his stare, from those intense, auburn brown eyes. I wanted to hate him so bad.

He was grinning, all smooth, with caramel brown skin that looked like the sun had kissed it. His dimples cut deep into his face when he smiled that smile. God had made him six feet tall with a head full of waves.

Then, I realized, something crazy. Nobody was even sitting back there with Shawn.

He had been talking to me the entire time, trying to get my attention. This boy, I laughed.

"You don't care about this class at all?" I asked.

He stretched, his arms flexing beneath an oversized hoodie on his athletic build.

"Not even a little bit. I don't need it." He replied.

"I do. Now be quiet." I rolled my eyes, and I faced forward, but the damage was done.

"And respect your elders," I said sternly.

Shawn leaned forward and whispered, "I got your attention though. The study queen has finally acknowledged my presence. Took you long enough."

I was confused, so I looked back at him.

"You never looked at me a day in your life," I said.

"Aht, aht. You are Ebony's friend and always look so damn mean. And the prettiest girls always have a mean dad, a big brother that can fight, or an attitude."

I laughed and whispered back. "You are wrong."

He moved closer to whisper in my ear. "Good, because. I was about to file a missing person's report for this conversation. I was trying to decide should I keep it professional, or risk it all." He said.

Professor Davis stopped speaking and looked at us. I felt Shawn move back. For a minute he was quiet, and then he said, "By the way, I am…"

I laughed and replied. "Trust me, I know who you are!"

"So you have ignored me this entire time just to make me work for it. Smart. I respect the hustle, even though I might be your new favorite person. I thought I would have to pass a note, like in middle school." He replied.

And just like that I met Shawn. Shawn Shawn.

I always said his full name, Shawn Jonathan Conquest. That's what Ebony called him.

To be smart, she would say it like Joe-Nathan, because he sometimes had a slight Southern accent. Wait, until I tell her about this morning.

Shawn was impossible to ignore after that. Aries men, I soon learned, are usually hard to ignore…

Teenage Love Affair...

Shawn and I—me, whatever—became friends before I even realized it was happening. I have never been a people person, so I must not have been paying attention. He had that effect on you.

He would ask to see my notes in class when he wasn't paying attention, or always asking to borrow a pen or a pencil, or saying silly stuff, like Will Smith's character on the TV show, "The Fresh Prince of Bel-Air."

"How tall do you think Jesus was in sandals?"

"How do they know what dinosaurs sound like? Like what if they talked like us?"

Just silly. Fun. And I won't lie, I liked it. He was always listening to music. He knew every song by heart. It didn't matter how old it was. I would say something, and he would sing a relevant song lyric back. But he cannot sing. He tried. Bless his little heart.

He would pop up at my job with coffee and a snack when I worked late in the cafeteria or library. He would always treat me to lunch and get mad if I tried to pay him back. He'd claim he was just walking by.

I was broke but didn't want to seem like I was taking his money. When Ebony found out that we were friends, she also developed a soft spot for him.

That is the only way you could explain how she would let him steal her food. Shawn was the reason why her roommate was always pissed.

Shawn stayed banging on their door. Always.

He would knock on her room door first, upsetting her then-roommate, Karlise, and then, when he came by my room to study, he would take her Twizzlers, his favorite, out of her room and our other snacks out of mine, only to replace them days later. It was his thing.

Study sessions turned into late-night phone calls. I had to tell him to get off the phone. He was always on level 10 crazy. Or telling me about a movie or a song.

Quick jokes in class turned into long conversations about life like "What if the Earth is an alien prison?"

He was dead serious about that one.

He told me about growing up in Atlanta and about his older brother, Max, who was the "golden child" and had their mother's approval while Shawn got her side-eye.

"My Mom always said 'Maxie,' she never calls him 'Max,'" was the one who made 'the good choices,'" he admitted one night while we sat outside the library sharing a big bag of chips and soda. Mr. Silly had become vulnerable. "And I was the one who made the fast ones."

I raised an eyebrow, "Fast choices?"

He smirked, "You know! The kind that feels good now but comes back to bite you later." I knew what he meant. As he talked, he had a look I couldn't place.

My life had been the total opposite. Scared.

Shawn had a reputation that fit his last name. Girls on campus whispered about him, how he could have you falling in love by Friday and forgetting your name by Monday. Ebony warned me about him on day one.

"Listen to me, NeeNee," she said, wagging a manicured finger. "That man got more games than the NBA. You don't want to be his next season."

"Shawn? He plays too much. I am not interested," I assured her. And I meant it.

I didn't see what all of them saw in him anyway.

He was too damn silly to me. Okay, he is charming. Smart. Funny. But… Okay, I lied. He doesn't even like me, at least not like that. He can have anybody.

This is Shawn. Shawn Shawn. That Shawn.

As much as I tried to pretend otherwise, there were moments—little ones, fleeting ones—when Shawn looked at me in a way that made my heart skip a beat and that damn smirk. I don't know. He surprised me.

When his fingers brushed mine while he passed me a pen, I wondered what I would feel like if he touched me intimately. And when he smiled.

I wasn't about to be another name on his list. A notch on his belt. They can have him.

I thought about it. Shawn is Shawn. No way!

Ebony saw me watching him one day while he was in the gym playing a pickup game of basketball. He stopped and took his shirt off. I almost died.

He saw me, smiled that crooked smile, gestured with his hand for me to call him later, and then went back to the game. I smiled, even with my eyes. Ebony saw it.

"Girl, NeeNee, you can lie to yourself if you want, but if he looked at me like that, I'd give him two kids and a puppy. Be that dutiful wife and all. I wouldn't care if his breath stinks."

"His breath doesn't stink," I said quietly. I had been close enough to know. I was still staring at him. "And you and anybody else can have him. Shawn is Shawn."

At least, that's what I told myself. I blamed him for how I was starting to feel about him...

Kissing You...

"It" happened leading up to finals week, when sleep was a luxury, and stress was the only thing keeping most people awake. Then Shawn called me.

Shawn and I had been in my dorm room for hours, surrounded by books, highlighters, half-empty drinks, and food wrappers. I was exhausted.

My brain felt like it had reached its limit, and no amount of studying was going to make any of the classes any clearer. I had even gotten Shawn to take his classes seriously, and he got a B on the midterm.

Now, I was stressing.

Shawn was at complete ease.

He wasn't even at the least bit worried about failing. He was sitting on my bed with me, flipping through his notes like a magazine. I was even jealous that he knew the answer to every question I quizzed him on.

"You know," he said lazily, with that smirk, "we should take a break. Go do something for just a little bit."

I shot him a look, "And do what? We ate."

He smirked, "I don't know. Something fun."

I scoffed, "Shawn, I don't have time for fun."

"See, that's your problem," Shawn said, sitting up to take my book away, "You're always so serious. You are not going to fail. You are too smart for all of that."

"I am not serious," I protested.

Shawn gave me a look. That look. That smirk.

I sighed, "Fine. Maybe, a little."

He grinned. "Hello! You need to loosen up."

Before I could respond, he moved closer. His hand brushed my knee, startling even me.

The air in the room was electric after that.

It was subtle, but I felt it. Shawn looked at me.

There was an electricity humming between us, something unspoken, but undeniable.

His eyes locked on mine. Then he spoke.

"You ever think about us?"

He had been thinking about that one.

My heart did a little two-step. "Us?"

"Yeah," his voice was lower, more seductive.

"Like… if we weren't just friends. Like if, you know…"

I swallowed hard. Was he serious?

My brain screamed at me to play it off, to laugh like it was a joke. He was serious, though.

And my body? My body was betraying me.

If he made another move, he could get it.

Then Shawn leaned in slowly, giving me a chance to pull away, but I didn't. He had me.

And when his lips touched mine, it was soft.

It was a taste and he pulled back.

He licked his lips again, and kissed me again.

It could have been something right there…

But I knew better. This is Shawn. Shawn!

I pulled away, laughing like it didn't mean anything.

I said, "Nice try, Conquest. But I am not your next mistake. Let's get back to studying."

He smirked, but there was something else in his eyes.

Something I couldn't name at first.

I should have known then what it was.

Determination.

I should have walked away. I should have run.

Instead, I let him stay and picked up my book again. He gave me a side-eye glance.

I looked at Shawn, but he was already back to studying. Summer was coming anyway. Shawn was about to leave for the summer to work with his dad, and I would be working. He would be okay with his other women.

At some point, I sat at my desk to work on something else. When I turned around to say something to Shawn, I saw that he was asleep, so I left him there. He was tired. He looked so peaceful, so I let him sleep.

When I got tired, I just crawled into my bed, that same bed with him. He was in my room.

It was too late to send him back across campus. He looked up at me, half asleep. He put his arms around me and laid back down like he didn't have a care.

It wasn't even like that, but for the first time in a long time, I honestly felt safe with him. I didn't know why.

I took a deep breath and inhaled his clean scent, even after a long day. He smelled like fabric softener, and I laughed. Yes, the fabric softener with the bear on the bottle. Maybe that is what it was. I don't know.

I moved ever so slightly, and Shawn pulled me closer to his body a little tighter like he didn't want me to go. I didn't want to leave either. My only problem is, little did I know, that was the beginning of our end…

How Could You Call Her Baby...

Summer came, and Shawn did leave.

It had been months since Shawn kissed me. Shawn didn't text back like he used to when the semester started. I didn't see him that first week because we no longer had a class together, and I thought maybe it was for the best. I did miss him, though.

At first, I thought maybe he was just busy. After all, this is his senior year. But then I saw him.

He had let his hair grow out, curly on the top and faded on the sides. He looked good. He looked tanned, if that was possible. There was only one problem.

He was walking across campus with her. Keisha.

"I have never met a baby named Keisha. You only meet a Keisha fully grown," Ebony later said.

I knew that they grew up together. Their mothers were sorority sisters. They had to be close, but not this damn close. What was this?

I had seen her around, but I couldn't say she and I were friends. She pretended to have it like that. I didn't. She had a clique around her. Her sorority sisters and I only hung around Ebony. Keisha is the kind of girl who looks like she picked out her outfits a week in advance.

Light-skinned with long, perfectly laid hair and a different designer bag slung over her arm like it came with her birth certificate. Her face was like a bird.

Long face, pointy nose, and she had that air about her—the one that said she wasn't here for fun; she was here to secure a future that matched how she grew up.

I didn't want to judge her. I didn't even know her. You have to be careful about what you hear about a woman. Rumors either come from a man who can't have her, or a woman that can't compete with her.

And yet, she was holding Shawn's hand like she owned it. Then, I realized that she did. He was hers.

I stopped mid-step, my stomach twisting.

Ebony was walking beside me and noticed what had grabbed my attention. Her face scrunched up.

"Oh, hell no," she muttered, stopping in her tracks. "Please tell me that isn't who I think it is."

I didn't answer. I didn't move. Just stood there, watching them. What else could I do?

Keisha must've felt me staring because she looked my way, her eyes sweeping over me with a quick calculation. Then, she laughed a fake laugh, as if Shawn told her a joke, and Shawn finally saw me.

And just like that, I knew—she knew who I was. It was Shawn who looked at me differently. Had Shawn told her about me? He had to the way she immediately became so clingy at my presence. I didn't like it.

"Girl," Ebony said, lowering her voice, "I knew he was a hoe, but I didn't think he was a disrespectful hoe. What is this? Her? Keisha."

"We are just friends." That made Ebony give me a side-eye look like stop playing. She folded her arms. Her eyes locked on Shawn like she was two seconds from throwing something at him. Or busting Keisha in the head with a brick. Probably both knowing her.

Shawn and Keisha started walking towards us as if Keisha had told him to say hi to me. She wanted to mark her territory. Ebony was ready to say something. Ebony, being Ebony, was on "go time." She was upset.

I was waiting to see what he had to say.

For a minute, I thought he would walk by me like he didn't even know my name, as if I was just another face on campus like he used to be before we had class, and just then, Ebony stepped in front of them.

It was as if she had been reading my mind the entire time. It wasn't like she didn't know Shawn, too.

Me. I didn't know what she was about to do.

At this point, I was worried for all of us.

This is Ebony Ebony…

Alright…

Ebony spoke in a fake southern drawl, "Shawn Jonathan Conquest, as I live and breathe. Shawn, why is that you, sugar dumpling? I know school just started, but last semester you damn near lived in our dorm. Where have you been since school started?"

Ebony was talking, but Keisha looked at me.

Shawn laughed, in faking annoyance, "Hiding from you. You cut me short on my last supply of candy. Being all stingy and mean. I thought we were good."

Ebony looked at Keisha and Shawn, speaking seductively to Shawn, "You? Never! You keep playing with me, Shawn Joe-Nathan. Come see me…"

"Keep playing with me. You aren't tall enough to ride this ride, Ebony." Shawn said to matched her energy. "And you don't have to be so mean. You know I love you. And you know what they say about short girls?"

Ebony gave him that face, and asked "What?"

Shawn laughed and said, "You know! Short girls are so mean, because y'all are so close to hell and all."

I laughed, and so did Ebony.

We both missed him.

I know I did.

Shawn gave me a glance and a quick smile.

Shawn then stooped down to be smart and hugged Ebony. She pretended to push him off her and said, "Boy, you know you are fine, but don't get too close before I forget I am saved. I was about to throw my panties at you, but I don't have that kind of money to waste throwing away good underwear."

Ebony didn't give a damn at that point, as she was openly flirting with Shawn, "Now you see why I blocked your number for my own safety. You could talk a vegan into a cheeseburger."

Shawn even laughed. Then he looked at me for a second and hugged me.

It wasn't like he used to when we heard Keisha clear her throat. He quickly pulled back.

He looked at me with that mischievous smile and said, "NeeNee… this is Keisha?"

I didn't care if she was Keyshia Cole.

I looked at Ebony. I realized that it was too late. Ebony already had her lips poked out, and was staring at Keisha, and then, at Shawn.

Keisha waved at us, and her face lit up in a fake, surprised way.

It was like when a beauty contestant won a pageant. You know how a pageant winner fakes surprise. You know where they do that fake shit like they are about to cry, but she remembers all of the time it took to put on that makeup. So, she won't dare to touch her face.

So, it looks like she is using her palms to fan her face. I wanted to laugh, but I played it cool.

"Shawn has told me so much about you," she said while sizing me up. Being fake.

"That's funny," Ebony retorted, "Shawn hasn't said anything about you being with him."

Keisha, clearly intending to ignore Ebony, tightened her grip on Shawn's arm and spoke.

"We need to go, or we will be late." Keisha insisted.

Without another word, Shawn walked across the quad with Keisha, only stopping to look back at me.

He smiled that smile that I missed.

He shrugged, and then Keisha pulled him in even closer, securing her grip on him.

Ebony gasped, clutching her chest like she had been personally attacked. "Oh, she got me fucked up."

She hissed. "NeeNee, you want me to fight her? 'Because I will. With her bird-faced self."

I shook my head, still trying to process the sudden nausea clawing at my stomach. "No."

"He didn't even introduce me to her." she raged, her voice an octave higher. "How rude! Okay, I did have classes with her. He is playing in your face. That man was just up in our dorm all last semester, eating our snacks, laying on your bed, breathing your air—and now, he got a girlfriend? When was this?"

"I don't know," I chimed in.

"It ain't going to last," Ebony countered. "I still love him, though. My panties did almost slide down when he walked by. I won't lie. They were at my knees."

I started laughing.

Ebony laughed. "Did you smell him? Why does he always smell like fresh laundry? I am over it. I don't even want to talk about it."

I knew she was joking. Ebony might be sociable, but she didn't like everybody. She did keep her ear to the ground and knew about everything on campus. This blindsided her. I know it. And this was about Shawn.

Shawn Shawn. My Shawn. Our Shawn.

Ebony was not about to let this one go.

In a way, neither was I.

I wanted to know what happened?

And, even more so, why? How?

And with Keisha, though…

You Can Call Me Crazy...

Ebony didn't let it go. She was still talking about it when we got to the dining hall. She was still talking about it between bites of her food and sips of her drink.

Ebony was hotter than fish grease.

By now, you know how she is. Always on "go."

"Keisha, though," Ebony said as we sat down.

She lived for the drama. This was the drama.

"And you see how he was acting? He never stops talking. He barely said a word to you."

I looked at Ebony and said, "I know you are not talking. You did all of the fussing with him."

"This isn't about me," Ebony said with a harsh look.

I laughed out loud. "It doesn't matter."

Ebony stopped and gave me another look.

Was that pity I just saw? About Shawn?

"Oh, it matters. It matters, NeeNee, because you're about to do that thing you do, where you act like you don't care when we both know you do. You have feelings for that man. I do, too. He gets on my damn nerves. With his tall self. Going to play me like I am short. You see how he looked at me and hugged me."

I looked at Ebony, "Because you are short to him."

She looked at me and laughed.

"Girl, who says he's happy, and why her? He could have been my future ex-husband? Not hers".

I exhaled slowly, pressing my lips together. Ebony wasn't wrong. It did matter. I did care about him. I think. I don't know. I'm confused. But it mattered more that

Shawn was with her. I didn't want to break up a happy home if he was happy with her. I couldn't. I should have said something, but, he chose her.

I had watched them as they walked out of sight. Keisha tugged him closer, whispering something in his ear.

She had his attention.

Ebony had made a noise between a growl and an exasperated sigh, bringing me back to the present conversation. I was listening again.

"Oh, she is one of those girls." She said.

I turned to her, raising an eyebrow.

"What kind of girls?" I was curious.

"The kind that stays scheming'." Ebony replied. "I bet she got a five-year plan that involves bagging a man with potential. He isn't broke and plays basketball. She is planning on riding his success and his dick all the way to the altar. I need a copy of her playbook."

She sniffed. "She isn't slick."

I bit the inside of my cheek to keep from laughing.

"Shawn grew up with her. She might be nice if Shawn likes her. Have you ever gotten to know her?" I asked.

"I don't need to." Ebony countered.

Ebony lifted a dramatic hand to the sky.

"The spirit of discernment is upon me!"

I laughed, despite my feelings. "Ebony, stop."

"No, I'm serious." She said shaking her head. "She's the type that wants to be a basketball wife but ain't never touched a ball in her life, except his, maybe. She makes them dribble. Get it? Dribble. And girls like her? They ruin everything. You have seen her on campus."

I sighed, my chest feeling way too tight. "It's fine, Eb. He made his choice. It's fine."

Ebony stared at me for a long time, then exhaled sharply. "Fine?" She echoed. "Fine?"

"You know what? I won't even argue with you because I know how this will go. You're gonna act all unbothered, tell me you don't care, and then—"

My phone buzzed. I pulled it out. It was a text.

From Shawn: I miss you.

I stared at the screen, my throat tightening.

Ebony peered over my shoulder, read the message, and let out a slow, exaggerated gasp. She is being so dramatic. Then, she turned to me with the widest, most dramatic eyes I had ever seen on her.

"OH. HELL. NO! And you, NeeNee, you know you are fighting your feelings harder than a toddler fights sleep." Ebony said.

I just looked at her. Ebony glared back at me.

Ebony ignored me, "Yeah, I should be getting paid to be in this mess. And for what I am about to say, you should be cutting me a check. She will never be you, NeeNee. She thinks she is the main character in Shawn's life and girl, she isn't even on the show…"

I laughed. "He has Keisha now."

Ebony ignored me again, and continued on, "I'm going to start charging people for wasting my time. $5 per dumb ass decision that I gotta witness. And Shawn being with Keisha is one of them when he knows he has feelings for you. I see it. And you have feelings for him, but you both are too stubborn to see it…"

Where Will You Go...

It had been a long day, and I was still up listening to Babyface. A song called "Where Will You Go" that Shawn played so much I couldn't get it out of my head. It reminded me of him. Everything always did.

Shawn Jonathan Conquest. Shawn Shawn.

It is a song about love, regret, and longing.

In it, Babyface watches somebody he loves walk away, questioning where their love would go and what their future would be. They too started out as friends.

It captured how I felt about Shawn and my hopes and prayers that this "thing" with Keisha was just a "thing." I kept wondering if she was good to him.

Here I was thinking about a future with him. I buried my head in my pillow and screamed. I hope I didn't wake up anybody on my floor, especially not Ebony.

I was still trying to figure out when Keisha came into the picture. He texted me all summer, but his texts and calls only trailed off leading up to move-in day.

What happened? I just wanted spent time with him.

I figured he was busy, and it was a long trip from Atlanta to here. What about ten hours? Would his parents drive with him? Did he take the train or fly?

Then Keisha showed up. He was with her.

Did she feel the same way I felt about him?

His following text came in just after midnight.

Shawn: You up.

I stared at the screen, my thumb hovering over the keyboard. Ebony would have taken the phone from me and tossed it across the room.

His words sat there, heavy, pulling at something deep in my chest.

I missed him too.

I wanted to ignore it. Ignore him.

I should have ignored it. Ignored him.

My heart was already beating too fast, and my fingers moved before my brain could catch up.

So I texted him back.

Me: Go to sleep, Mr. Conquest.

It took him less than a minute to respond.

Shawn: I can't.

I hesitated. Lying felt pointless.

Me: Yeah. I am up.

Shawn: Good. I'm outside of your dorm.

I shot up in bed so fast that my sheets tangled around my legs. I almost fell off the bed and died, imagining Ebony finding me like that and because of Shawn.

I scrambled out of bed, heart pounding, and rushed to the window to take a look. He was there.

Sure enough, Shawn was leaning against a lamp post, his hands stuffed in his hoodie pocket, looking like he had all the time in the world.

How long had he been out there?

I wanted to be mad, but as he stood there towering over everything—I am only five feet six inches— I was happy to see him.

I wanted to ask him why he was here. Why was he texting me at almost one a.m. when he had a whole girlfriend?

He should be asleep.

He should be with her.

Instead, I grabbed a hoodie and sweatpants, got dressed, put on my sneakers, and slipped out the door.

He didn't speak when I stepped outside.

He tilted his head like he always did when he was figuring out what to say before he said it.

I was patient.

I hoped it wasn't bad news. That Keisha wasn't ready to jump out of the bushes and catch us together.

Like surprise! Gotcha! She looked like the type.

The night air was cool, but my skin was too hot, my pulse too wild. Then, he looked at me.

Shawn didn't say a word at first.

He reached out and grabbed my hand, and then he hugged me, like he used to do. It felt good.

I tried to step back, but he held me tighter, as if he was almost afraid to let me go. This was real. Not a dream.

So, I let him.

Big mistake.

I should have run like a track star.

Why I didn't? I don't know.

Finally, I stepped back. We needed to talk.

I wasn't ready for what happened next...

Just The Lonely Talking Again...

"What are you doing here, Shawn?" I asked, keeping my voice steady. Could he still tell I was nervous?

He exhaled. "I don't know. I asked myself that when I was walking over. I missed you, I guess."

He looked at the ground, and I believed in what he said for the umpteenth time since I met him.

"You don't know?" I questioned him. "You guess?"

He ran a hand over his face; there was a tension in his shoulders that I wasn't used to seeing in him.

"Keisha and I got into it again. I'm so tired. She is burning me out. I am cooked." He confessed.

"What does that have to do with me?" I asked.

"She is feeling some strange way about my relationship with you? She saw my text." He answered.

I looked at him, wanting him to continue.

"She thinks I have feelings for you, like I make everything about you and me. I told her I needed to study, and she asked why now? I told her you stayed on me to ensure I learned something last semester. You did that. I think she is jealous of you, of us."

"Doesn't she know that we are just friends?" I asked, knowing I was lying the minute I said the words. "I care about you, but you are with Keisha, and that's where you need to be. I am not trying to get in the way of that."

"She doesn't believe me. And I don't want to keep going through this with her. Her Mom and my Mom are still trying to do that bullshit where they put us together again. I worked with her all last summer. And then, something happened. I said forget it, and I gave in."

He gave in? He fucked her. That's what he meant.

I folded my arms. "And what? You thought I'd make you feel better about this? I wouldn't know how."

His jaw flexed. "Damn, NeeNee. You are my best friend. Can you help me out? Just listen."

Best friend? I only ever had Ebony... until him.

I ignored his words, even though I felt them. Out of all the people he knew, he was around and spent time with, he chose me over everyone else he knew?

And then, I gave him grace that, maybe, he has had to question his entire life, like if the people around him had been around him because of who he is and what he has, over what kind of person he is deep inside.

"What do you want me to say?" I challenged. "You pulled back, got a whole girlfriend, and now you're standing outside my dorm like—"

"Like I miss you," he said, his voice was rough. "Like I don't know how to do this without you in my life."

I hated how my chest tightened when he said that.

I hated how much I wanted to believe him.

"Do what, Shawn?" I was confused.

"Everything. You understood me since the beginning. At least, that's what I felt. That was enough for me. It's not like that with her. I don't know why I am with her."

His eyes met mine, and it wasn't just words. He felt everything he was saying. I was it in his eyes as he continued. This was a different Shawn than who I met.

"I'm about to graduate, and then, what? Until you came along, I didn't take school seriously. My coach made sure we passed. Then, you showed up. You made me want to do more, be better, do better. You made me love myself a little more. I needed that. I needed you."

He looked at me and smirked that smirk.

It was real. "You've been my best friend since the first day of class, and then, we kissed, and I thought I fucked that up, for real. I don't know how to fix this between us. I don't want to lose what we have."

"Fix what?" I asked, suddenly curious.

"Fix how I feel about you. I thought I broke us," He said. "NeeNee, I—I don't know anymore. How I feel about you is no longer an option. How I feel about you brings out the best and the worst in me."

I swallowed hard, my resolve slipping. "That's what happens when you start dating a girl who doesn't even know me, but she hates me."

"She doesn't hate you." He didn't know.

87

I shot him a look and laughed. "I heard her earlier, after I met her, with her clique. As I walked by, she called me 'that girl.' Like who does she think she is?"

He sighed, shaking his head. "Keisha doesn't get us. We are different. You are the first girl who doesn't care about anything, but if I am good. If I ate? How was my day? You listen to me when I talk. I needed that. You see me. Even in the dark, you'd find me. You get me."

"She doesn't have to get us," I said, my voice sharper than I intended. "You made your choice."

Silence stretched between us, thick and full of things we weren't saying. Shawn looked at me again.

My heart broke for him. This is Shawn pouring his heart out to me. He is a man that I used to be unable to take seriously at one point. And yet, I was right here.

This is that Shawn. Did the boy once ask me how tall I thought Jesus was, with and without a pair of sandals?

The same person who professed that he wanted to be a stripper at some point in his life and found every opportunity to dance. When I asked him what he wanted, he would say to try crack cocaine, as a joke.

And me, being silly, would do my impression of Mr. Joe Clark in the movie, "Lean On Me." Saying "You want to smoke crack don't' you." It's like that with him.

Then, he would do his best imitation of the interview with Whitney Houston and Diane Sawyer, saying "crack is cheap." That "crack is whack" and how we don't do crack. He makes too much money to ever smoke crack. See. Silly. That was Shawn.

That wasn't the person standing here now.

Then, Shawn stepped closer. Too close.

The scent on his hoodie—something fresh, something clean—wrapped around me.

It was that damn fabric softener like that night in my room when I crawled into bed with him after he kissed me.

His eyes dropped to my lips, and every nerve in my body lit up like fireworks.

"This wasn't supposed to be complicated," he murmured. "I miss you, NeeNee."

I swallowed. My pulse was hammering. "Then why are you making it complicated?"

I learned to hate that word because of him.

Shawn licked his lips in a way that only he could. His voice did a slow burn against my skin. I almost forgot where we were. That this man did not belong to me.

"I'm not. I don't want to lose you if we do something we can't take back. Tell me to stop, and I will. No doubts. No regrets. Even if it is for one night. You know how I feel about you." He pressed his body against mine.

I felt it. I felt him. I felt dizzy.

His fingers brushed mine. Barely.

Just enough to make me shiver.

"Do you say this to all of your chicks?"

"No. Even when I was with Keisha, it's you."

My breath hitched. "Shawn…"

But he was already moving.

One hand on my waist, the other sliding up my arm until he reached for my face, fingers ghosting over my skin like a question.

I should have stopped him.

I should have turned away and reminded him that we were just friends, that he had a girlfriend, and that this was a bad idea. I didn't give a fuck. Forget her.

I didn't stop him.

Instead, I closed my eyes as his lips brushed mine.

Soft.

Slowly.

Then deeper. I felt his kiss, and it was electric.

It was better than the first time we kissed.

Finally, I whispered. "One time, and we never talk about this again. Once! Deal?"

Shawn laughed, "You say that now, but deal."

A groan rumbled in his chest as his grip tightened, pulling me flush against him. I felt everything—every moment we spent pretending, every joke, every lingering look, every "almost" that led us to right now.

The kiss wasn't just a kiss.

It was a confession about how he felt.

And I kissed him back like it was my answer...

Ready For Love...

My back hit the wall of my dorm the second we stumbled inside. We both laughed at that.

His hands were everywhere—palms tracing my waist, fingers tangled in my hair.

My breath came in short gasps as his mouth trailed from my lips to my neck, and I melted, letting him press me into the closed door.

"Tell me to stop," he murmured against my skin. "Tell me to leave."

I should have. I wanted to. I am lying.

Looking into his eyes, I saw the same thing I felt— need, longing, something more profound than we were ready for. He touched me like he knew my body.

So, instead, I pulled him closer. "No."

He won. He took his prize.

I wanted it. I wanted him.

And Shawn didn't stop.

He became my first...

As We Lay...

The room was quiet afterward. Our breathing was the only sound, except for the birds outside my window. I looked at the time—it was early in the morning.

Shawn lay beside me in the twin bed, staring at the ceiling, his arm draped over his forehead. We had done it twice. It was good both times.

It finally happened.

I should have felt guilty.

I should have said something.

Instead, I just watched him, memorizing how the lights outside streamed through my blinds, painting shadows across his face.

After a long moment, he spoke.

"That shouldn't have happened."

I stiffened. "Yeah. I guess."

He turned to look at me, "We both wanted it. I wanted you. You wanted me, but it was..."

His voice trailed off, trying to find the words.

"A mistake," I finished the thought for him.

His sat up quickly and said, "I didn't say that."

I sat up, wrapping the sheet around me. "You didn't have to. You will never be mine."

"NeeNee—"

I swung my legs off the bed, grabbing my clothes off the floor. "You should go."

He ran his hands over his face. "Damn. It's like that? We need to talk. Can we do that first?"

I swallowed against the ache in my chest.

"Keisha's probably looking for you."

Silence. He knew the truth. She is possessive.

Then, quietly, he said, "Probably."

I nodded, biting my lip to keep it from trembling. There was so much I wanted to say.

"Then go," I said instead.

Shawn hesitated as if he wanted to say something else but didn't.

He just gave me a look I'd never seen before. It seemed like his Mom was right—he was too impulsive. This was another bad decision.

He didn't need to say it. I felt it, though.

He took a deep breath, got up, grabbed his clothes, and slowly dressed. He didn't even look at me.

I didn't watch him leave. I already allowed myself to forget that he doesn't belong to me.

I didn't want to see his face. I just wanted to remember having him, even for a moment. I wanted to hold on to this moment's memories, not the pain.

I didn't move until I heard the soft click of the door.

He was gone. Finally. Like what did we do?

Then, and only then, did I let the tears fall.

I was so confused. How could we be friends after this?

Had I lost Shawn, too?

Maybe I did this to push him away.

Nothing I could do would change the fact that he was with Keisha. She is his girlfriend.

Not me. I wish I was.

That is his choice to leave her or to stay.

Right now, that's where he needed to be, and I was good with that. Or was I just lying to myself...

Didn't We Almost Have It All...

The morning after was the worst part. I woke up tangled in my sheets, my body still humming with the feelings of last night. I could still smell him on my covers.

But it was like Shawn was never even really here.

I could still smell him on my skin.

My lips tingled, like they still carried the weight of his kisses, and my skin felt too hot, too aware of the mistake I had made. My desire for him was still strong.

I told myself it didn't mean anything.

I told myself I wouldn't think about him.

Then my phone vibrated on the desk. I checked it.

Shawn: You good?

I closed my eyes and exhaled.

I should've ignored it.

Pretended last night never happened.

But my fingers moved before my brain could stop them.

Me: Yeah. Are you good?

Shawn: I didn't go to sleep yet.

A pause. Then another text.

Shawn: We should talk. Breakfast?

My stomach tightened.

Talking meant facing the reality that we did it.

And reality meant acknowledging that I had slept with an off-limits man in ways I didn't even have the energy to unpack. At least, not right now. I was confused.

Me: No, we shouldn't. It was one time.

I turned my phone off before he could respond.

Then, like she had a radar for my bullshit, Ebony burst into my room without knocking.

"Okay, you got some explaining to do!"

I barely had time to process her presence before she jumped onto my bed, narrowing her eyes like she was scanning me for evidence of something nefarious.

"You look..." She tilted her head. "Suspicious!"

I rolled my eyes and pulled the blanket over my head. "Ebony, please—"

"Nope." She snatched the covers back.

"You didn't answer my texts last night when I saw you outside with whoever that was, and now you're in here looking like you just got your soul snatched. Back blown out." Then she stopped suddenly.

She squinted. "Oh my God! You did!"

I stayed silent, hoping she'd let it go. Nope!

Ebony gasped, smacking my arm. "NeeNee! Who was it? Was it Ronnie? Bobby? Ricky? Mike? Ralph?"

Then, her eyes widened. "Wait… oh, hell no! Sweet baby Jesus! Mary and Joseph!"

She stopped and smelled the air again.

I flopped onto my back, covering my face with my hands. I was embarrassed. She knew.

Silence, then, she said, "What the devil?"

I peeked through my fingers. "Ebony—"

She leaned in like I had just confessed to murder. "You slept with him? Shawn!? Joe-Nathan."

"I didn't plan it. It just happened."

"Oh, so you accidentally landed on his dick?"

I groaned as Ebony pretended to look around the room to see precisely what I tripped on. "I can smell him, girl. That damn fabric softener. It hypnotized you."

Ebony flopped onto my bed dramatically. "Girl, and it is community dick. All of these thirsty chicks want that man. Then, you know his girlfriend is crazy. What did I tell you? He almost got me too. I heard about it."

"I know. It is okay. It was a one-time thing."

She sat up. "What the hell are you gonna do? I hope it was worth it that you let that man rearrange your spine like a chiropractor."

"Nothing," I muttered. "I'm going to forget it happened and move on. He will be okay."

Ebony sniffed. "Yeah, good luck with that. If you try to block him, he will pop up in your dreams. We are talking about Shawn Shawn, and y'all are messy as hell. And I want to say, as an innocent bystander, I support it."

I laughed, "Thank you, Ebony."

Then Ebony got very serious. Or at least, I thought she was about to be.

"This is some "Scandal"-type shit," she said, "And I don't know if I am supposed to be Olivia Pope and help you to fix this shit, or I am in the audience and gasping at what I am watching unfold…"

Go On Without You…

I spent the rest of the day avoiding my thoughts, keeping my phone on silent, and convincing myself everything would be fine. He would go back to Keisha.

We're good. We agree it was a one-time thing.

Then I saw him.

Ebony was right. Dammit, Ebony! This is so messy!

I wanted him. Did I have real feelings for him?

I was walking across campus when Shawn stepped out of the gym and pulled his hoodie over his head. His eyes swept the crowd, searching for something. Or someone. Was he looking for me?

He must've been leaving practice. He looked different to me, as if he had a lot on his mind.

The second he saw me, my pulse stuttered.

He smiled like he was genuinely happy to see me. This is the person that I… know.

He started toward me, and for a second, I thought about running, but I didn't want to.

But a sharp voice sliced through the air before we could say a word.

"There you are!" As Keisha appeared.

I turned, moving like she owned the sidewalk, walking towards Shawn and me. I should have left.

Silly me, I froze, but she already saw me, which is why she was making such a scene. I figured as much.

She walked up to Shawn, linking her arm through his to make a point. "Why weren't you answering my calls, Sugar Bear?" Sugar Bear? Who the fuck is that?

Shawn's whole body tensed, his jaw tightening. "I was busy. My phone was in my bag, and I was at practice. Why? What's up?"

Keisha pouted. "Since last night? Strange."

I should've left them to this conversation.

I should've walked away before she noticed me looking at the two of them. It was too late.

Her eyes landed on me, and her expression shifted like she sensed what we did. How?

"Oh," she said, voice dripping with fake sweetness. "Hey, NeeNee."

I forced a response. "Hey, Keisha."

Her gaze flickered between me and Shawn, her lips curling just slightly.

"You look tired," she said, tilting her head.

"Rough night?" She was faking her concern.

My stomach twisted. She looked at Shawn.

Shawn stiffened beside her, but I caught that flicker of something in his eyes, so I played my part.

She knew. Or at least, she suspected.

I cleared my throat. "Just a lot on my mind."

Keisha's smirk deepened. "Mmm. Maybe you need to get some rest then, NeeNee."

She squeezed Shawn's arm, her nails digging in just enough to make another point. "You don't want to be looking so… like an old alley cat."

I forced a tight smile. "I'm good."

She stared at me for a moment too long, her expression undeniable. She didn't like me.

Then, just as quickly, she turned back to Shawn with an exaggerated cheerfulness.

"Come on, baby. Let's go."

Shawn didn't move at first.

His eyes lingered on me, something unspoken hanging between us. He wanted to talk to me.

Keisha tugged his arm. "Now."

He exhaled and let her pull him away.

I watched them go, my skin burning under Keisha's gaze as she glanced back at me, and then, again one last time.

That wasn't a look of curiosity.

It was a warning.

She wasn't just suspicious.

She knew something happened, but not what.

Or she pretended to know.

And she was about to make sure I knew that whatever was going on with Shawn, she wasn't having any of that foolishness. Ebony came out of nowhere.

She must have seen the whole exchange. She looked at me and reiterated what she said before.

"I told you she was mean-spirited. She wakes up mad. And about Shawn, she would have beefed with the wind if it blew past him. Please don't take what she says and does personally; she doesn't even like herself. Let her be great."

And Ebony walked away without another word…

Somebody's Watching Me...

I told myself I was being paranoid.

Keisha didn't know anything and was her usual passive-aggressive, territorial self.

Ebony said to ignore her.

But as the days passed, I couldn't shake the feeling that she was watching me.

And then, she made it obvious.

It started small. And by small, Keisha was acting weird.

Days after I ran into her and Shawn, I stopped by my favorite coffee shop before class. As I waited in line, I felt that weird, prickling sensation of being watched.

I glanced over my shoulder.

There she was. Keisha.

Sitting by the window, sipping an iced coffee, her eyes locked on me like a sniper.

She raised her cup in a slow, deliberate toast.

I turned back around and pretended not to see her.

It wasn't very smart of me to even try.

She already acknowledged me.

The next day, it was the library.

I was minding my business, highlighting notes, when a shadow fell over my table.

"Didn't take you for the studious type."

I looked up. Keisha. She lied so easily.

She knew Shawn, and I studied together.

She leaned against the table.

I forced a tight smile. "You need something?"

"No, I was just... noticing things." She dragged her acrylics along the wooden surface of the table. The sound was making my skin itch. "Like how Shawn has been acting a little... off."

I blinked. "Off?"

She leaned in slightly. "Jumpy. Avoiding eye contact. Looking guilty like a bad dog."

And she was his bitch.

My pulse kicked up, but I kept my face neutral.

"Sounds like you're seeing things."

She let out a low chuckle. "Maybe."

Then, after a beat, "You know, women always know, NeeNee, even when men lie. Even when they try to be slick. We know. This thing with Shawn is getting weird."

My fingers tightened around my pen. She is weird.

She was stupid. How would she know Shawn cheated?

What did he do? He couldn't have outright told her. Shawn wasn't like that. Did he try a new position that he learned with me on her? We did do it twice.

She gave me a slow, knowing smile. "I'll be seeing you around. Hopefully not around Shawn."

And just like that, she walked off, her heels clicking against the floor like the beat of a war drum.

By the weekend, I was convinced she was setting me up for something. A fight, maybe?

I told Ebony about it later. Of course, she found the whole thing entertaining, and almost silly.

"Okay, so let me get this straight," she said between bites of her Chinese takeout.

"Keisha has been popping up on you like she is the Secret Service, hitting you with subliminal threats and dramatic-ass exits? Girl, bye!"

"Yes." I groaned. "And it's freaking me out."

Ebony cackled. "Girl, you ain't built for this toxic shit. I need you to beat her natural Black ass."

I felt like I heard somebody say that before years ago.

"No, I am not." I put my food down. Suddenly, I had lost my appetite thinking about this. Was it worth this?

She grinned, "You gotta admit, though—this is kinda exciting. All of this sneaking around."

I shot her a look. "Exciting? Girl, bye!"

"Yeah! It's like a real-life soap opera. You got the sneaky affair, the crazy girlfriend, the suspense." She wiggled her fingers dramatically. "The danger. The drama. But if Keisha ever looks at you wrong, it's on."

I sighed. " Thank you, but, Ebony—it was one night."

"You need to relax then," she said, waving me off. "Keisha ain't got no proof. She's just fishing."

"Maybe."

"Definitely." Ebony replied. "Now eat your food."

I wanted to believe her. I really did. Then, again, Keisha wasn't wrong. I did the damnedest thing; I slept with her man, though.

In a way, Shawn and I gave each other the better parts of ourselves. He will always be my first.

And now, I wanted to do it again. So I texted Shawn…

My Little Secret...

One time was a mistake, but by the fourth time, I knew I had made a decision. Crack may be whack, but Shawn became my drug of choice and I was hooked.

Shawn and I had fallen into a rhythm, a dangerous and addictive rhythm with sex. We weren't together, and we weren't apart either. We were seeing what could be.

You know.

Somewhere between "this is a mistake" and "we can't stop," we created our own little world.

One that only existed in the sheets, in the late-night phone calls, and how he looked at me like I was his whole universe when he thought I wasn't looking.

I was looking. I knew how he made me feel.

And I wasn't stopping it. I didn't want to stop it.

We didn't want it to stop.

Even after everything with Keisha, even after I told myself to put walls up, I kept letting Shawn back in. We would do it again to get it out of our system.

"This was the last time, NeeNee," I would say.

The next thing you know; Shawn would text me. We did it in his room. In my room. The library. I was lying to myself. Every. Single. Time.

And I wasn't the only one who noticed.

I wasn't good at sneaking. I could never rob a bank.

That's how we got caught.

I got caught.

By Ebony.

It was six in the morning this last time, and the last thing that I needed was to hear Ebony's mouth after another night with Shawn. I told Ebony I was going to bed.

I snuck out and met Shawn. I barely got to my door after creeping past Ebony's dorm room.

Her lights were out. Good.

I didn't hear her. Hopefully, she was asleep.

I was holding my breath as I stepped inside my room.

The room was dark and quiet.

Too quiet.

Then I heard it. Clap. Clap. Clap. I froze.

"So, how was it?" She asked like a TV villain.

I damn near jumped out of my skin as I flicked on the light. "Ebony, what is wrong with you?"

Ebony had been sitting in the dark, looking like a concerned, but angry parent waiting for her wayward and disobedient child to sneak back into the house.

She was so dramatic. She was sitting on my bed, arms crossed, bonnet slightly lopsided, looking too pleased with herself. I was busted. I knew it. She knew it.

So I did what I could do and turned it back on her.

"What's wrong with me?" She tilted her head. "Oh, nothing; I was waiting for my trifling best friend to come slinking here. Did you even wash your ass before you left him?"

I scowled and turned away, fumbling with my hoodie zipper. "Mind your business. And yes, I did!"

"Oh, it is my business when you keep sneaking off like you got a second family. And I was just checking."

Then, I stopped… "Wait! How did you get in?"

"Girl, how do you think? I am from Brooklyn! You don't know how many times I got locked out of my building. That is not the point. By the way, I borrowed your curlers again. I didn't have time to bring them back."

I rolled my eyes and said it, "You're so dramatic."

Ebony gasped and clutched her face like I just slapped her. "Dramatic? Me? Oh no, baby. You are the one living a whole double life? NeeNee, Double O'hoe."

She laughed at her own joke. She then tapped her chin, pretending to think and said, "Let's see, who could you

110

possibly have you leaving at midnight and strolling in at six in the morning? Looking all suspicious and glowing? Let me see... Is it a Mr. Shawn Conquest?"

I sucked my teeth. "Girl, go to bed."

She ignored me and grinned. "Wait, hold up. Don't tell me... It is Shawn, ain't it?"

I whipped around so fast that I nearly tripped over my own two feet. I gave her that look.

Ebony's jaw dropped. "Oh, bitch. Spill it."

"Lower your damn voice."

"I knew it. I knew y'all was creeping, but now he got you dickmatized. Does it do tricks?"

I let out a long sigh.

"Okay, yes. Fine. It's Shawn. Now go to bed," I said.

Ebony jumped up like she won the lottery.

"I knew it! Finally! Is it good good?"

I couldn't help it, so I burst out laughing.

"Yes, now stop," I replied, but the damage was already done. If Ebony knew, then who else knew?

Ebony cackled. "Oh, this is so messy. I love it. Okay, so are y'all together? Friends with benefits? Or is this a "D" appointment situation? Like, does he drop it off on you, say thank you, and keep it pushing?"

I hesitated because, in truth, I didn't know.

Shawn and I never talked about what we were doing. We just did it. I was good with that.

It felt good, and it felt right. I wanted this.

Every single time, I told myself it was the last time, and then, somehow, I'd find myself back in his bed. Back in his arms. Back with him.

Ebony leaned in, suddenly serious. "Do you love him? I mean, does he love you?"

I swallowed. Of course, I do. I think he does.

We just never talked about it.

Now, thinking about it? That was different.

That meant I'd have to do something about it.

So, instead, I shrugged, "It does not matter."

Ebony gave me a knowing look, "You are a damn liar, and you need to teach me how to lie, when you locked down the biggest player on campus. This is Shawn Jonathan Conquest! Girl, I am jealous of you."

I scoffed. And laughed. "And?"

She smiled and nudged me.

"Fine, fine. But let me say this—at least let me be your maid of honor when you finally admit you are in love with this man and get married."

"You want to fight, huh?" I asked.

"You will be fighting when Keisha finds out."

Ebony laughed as she got up to leave.

Was I really playing house with Shawn... Or was I already home? How did I feel?

Then, I looked at myself in the mirror, and it happened just as I was about to get in bed.

I wanted to say it was my nerves, but I threw up...

Baby, Baby, Baby...

I stared at the stick in my hand, my pulse thudding so hard, I could hear it in my ears.

This can't be happening. Not now. Nope.

The first chance I got, I ran to get a pregnancy test.

Okay, you know what I mean, I walked.

I was praying nobody saw me, too.

Especially not Ebony. Not Shawn. Not Keisha.

I would never hear the end of it.

We should have used protection.

Shawn did get tested regularly. I was a virgin.

A disease was the least of our worries.

The sex was just so random. We just did it.

Looking at the test, I closed my eyes and opened them again, unsure of what to do.

Two pink lines. Positive.

I squeezed my eyes shut again and counted to ten. When I opened them, I prayed it would be different.

Like sike! No baby!

Maybe my body was playing tricks on me.

Maybe I had been stressing too much.

Now that has happened before.

I have never been this late, though.

I thought I was being careful with the days.

I looked again. Still positive.

I let out a slow, shaky breath and dropped the test on the counter like it had burned me.

This cannot be happening. Not now. Not like this.

I gripped the edge of the sink, nausea rolling through me—not from morning sickness, but pure panic.

I am pregnant. Like pregnant pregnant.

And I had no idea what the hell I was going to do. I didn't know how to be a mother.

The one that birthed me never even showed me what a mother was supposed to look like. Shit, I was just learning how to be me. I have to tell Ebony!

She would know exactly what to do…

To Make A Long Story Short...

"Girl, I don't know what to do!" Ebony shrieked!

Ebony, at that point, had to pull her car over.

"NeeNee, do NOT play with me right now."

"You know how to handle everything else," I said as I sat frozen in the passenger seat, staring out the window like I wished I could disappear into the sky.

"I normally do, but can I get a break?" Ebony said, sucking her teeth. "Are you even sure sure? I mean, stop playing. For real, for real."

"I took the test earlier when you were at work." I said. "Then, I said I need to tell Ebony. She will know what to do. Personally, I think you are holding back."

"See, this is why I drink. Stress. I need a drink," Ebony replied. "Oh wait, you can't drink now. Now I gotta drink for two. This is exhausting. NeeNee... girl!"

I laughed. Ebony looked at me and laughed, too.

This shit wasn't funny, though.

Ebony smacked the steering wheel. "Ain't no damn way. Didn't I teach you better than this?"

"Bitch, way," I replied. "And you did! You tried."

She blew out a breath and shook her head.

"Damn, girl." She glanced at me, her face unreadable. Ebony then looked at me like she was my mother and took a deep breath. "I honestly don't know what to do about this and what to do with you."

Silence filled the car. It was as thick as concrete.

"I am sorry, Ebony." Then, I got quiet.

"NeeNee," Ebony's voice was kinder now, less dramatic. "Was it Shawn? At least tell me that."

I nodded. Damn. I hadn't even said his name out loud. Telling him wasn't even on my mind.

"He was my first," I said quietly.

Just then, Ebony's facial expression changed.

"Bitch, I thought you said you were almost a Virgo. Not a virgin. Now, this complicates everything. You let Shawn Shawn, with his tall drink of water ass and caramel skin, shoot the club up. He was supposed to have been mine. Is this what the hell we're doing?"

I wanted to laugh at Ebony's silliness.

"Ebony, you are making it worse." I laughed.

"At least we get to throw a gender reveal and not a Maury watch party for this baby." Ebony said. "I can see you now trying to run from that camera man. You will not get far. That man can run like it's the Olympics."

Ebony had jokes. I swallowed hard, my stomach twisting into a knot. I had made my bed. Now I was laying in it, lying in it, with Shawn Jonathan Conquest.

I didn't have to describe him. Everybody knew him. I knew he was going to be trouble. He is like a cold or the flu. He sneaks up on you. That's how he got me.

Then Ebony let out a slow whistle.

"You sure you are pregnant, or is your uterus holding a grudge? Aunt Flo can be a bitch. And if this baby's first words aren't Aunt Ebony is the best, it's going back."

I laughed. "You know you are crazy, right?"

Ebony looked at me, laughed, and drove off without looking at me again. I looked out the window.

"So what's the plan? You gonna tell him?'"

I hesitated. "I don't know yet."

"What do you mean 'You don't know yet.'"

I exhaled. "I mean, I don't know. He has a girlfriend. Keisha's already suspicious. If she finds out I'm pregnant? Oh, it's over for the both of us."

Ebony shot me a look. "Girl, it was over the moment you let Shawn flip you like a pancake, and now you got a whole bun in the oven. Fuck that bitch."

I groaned and slumped in my seat. "Not helping. I thought I was a big girl. It was just so good."

Ebony laughed at me, saying, "You cannot even write him a note like 'I'm pregnant' and leave it on his windshield. That man will be analyzing the shit, like the FBI's crime lab, with a suspect board. Calling his boys, Bobby and Frank, to run a full investigation. Is this NeeNee's cursive, or is Keisha setting him up?"

Even I had to laugh. Ebony laughed, too.

"I'm just saying." She sighed. "Look, I get it. It's messy. But that doesn't change the facts. If you're pregnant, he's the father. He deserves to know. Shawn is Shawn, but Shawn is still a good man. I love him. I love him for you. I think he will be okay with this."

I swallowed hard. My throat was dry. "And then what? Does he leave Keisha? He steps up? Or worse—he says nothing changes, and I'm stuck raising a baby alone? I don't know. People change about a baby."

Ebony thought about it. "You are right. I get it."

Ebony was quiet, then said, "But you're not gonna be alone. Either way. If you choose to tell him or not. I am here, girl. Where am I going? And my Nana."

I looked at her. She knew how my Mom used me to get my Dad to marry her. Look how that turned out anyway.

I wasn't doing that shit to Shawn. How could I?

"Thank you. You are the best." I smiled.

She rolled her eyes. "Duh. You think I'm about to let you do this by yourself? Please. I'll be the best damn fake baby daddy you ever had. Watch me."

In a fake deep voice, she said, "Be at the daycare like 'I am here to pick up my baby.'"

A loud laugh bubbled up in my throat, and for the first time that day, the crushing weight on my chest lifted—just a little.

"Thanks, B." She knew I meant it.

"Anytime. You know I got your back, girl."

I hadn't noticed that she drove us to a pharmacy until she pulled into a parking spot, and cut the engine.

I was still lost in thought.

"Now come on. We got work to do." Ebony said.

I frowned. "What work?"

She snatched her purse up, and looked at me like I should know. "We gotta buy more tests."

I groaned. "Ebony, I already told you. I'm pregnant."

"Oh, hush. We are confirming this again before we have a full-blown breakdown. Some tests are wrong."

I sighed and followed her inside, knowing she wasn't letting this go. Ebony never lets anything go.

"Besides," she started again, "We know Shawn. He would never be one of those men who makes a baby, and then, lets you find another man to care for it. That's not him. He might make a damn good father and husband. And you a phenomenal mother and wife."

"And," she continued, "Shawn won't get mad at you about this. Be like 'this bitch.' The only time a man calls a woman a bitch is when she broke his heart, he can't have her, or she rejected him. He loves you, and you love him. That will be all that matters to him."

Ebony was still talking, "And from what you told me, Shawn loves his mother. What I have learned is a man that loves his mother, and I mean truly loves her, would never treat any other woman like anything but the queen she deserves to be. Real men are like that."

"If he calls his mother, or any woman, a bitch, what makes you think you aren't next? And if he treats his mother good, but you bad, that is a red flag. That's 'Mommy issues.' Some deep-rooted, emotional trauma from his childhood relationship with his mother. Or a problem with healthy relationships with women."

I was only half listening. As much as I wanted to pretend this wasn't real... I am pregnant. I was about to be somebody's mother. Where was mine?

Or, at least, I might be someone's mother.

But it is Shawn's baby.

And no matter how much I tried to ignore it I couldn't hide from this forever...

Hoping, Wishing, Praying…

The trip to the store was a disaster before it even started. I realized it confirmed the situation. Ebony did not help. My best friend is crazy. Crazy crazy.

And she wasn't even drinking.

Once in the store, Ebony was too excited.

"Why are you so nervous?" she asked as we walked in.

I didn't answer. Damn if I know. So I shrugged.

She grinned. "Girl, you look like you are waiting for a job interview. Bring your ass on."

I tried to keep my head down as we walked to the pregnancy test aisle. They had a test for everything. Paternity. Marijuana. Damn.

I was still cautious. When you try to do things quietly, everybody and their mother will see you, like "Hey girl."

Ebony went and grabbed a basket.

"What is the basket for?" I called out.

"In case we need something else. I don't know how to change a damn diaper. Get a pack."

Ebony then looked at me when she came down the aisle, seeing me trying to act normal. Cool and natural, I guess. "Girl, who are you hiding from? If we run into somebody we know, I will pretend this is for me."

I laughed and said, "Damn if I know and you do that."

I was just trying to be discreet, but Ebony, being Ebony, made it damn near difficult.

She picked up a box and waved it in the air, "This one says it is clinically proven to be 99% accurate. Do you want that, or the cheap one? I say we go with this one."

I snatched it out of her hand and hissed at her. "Do not announce it to the whole store?"

She shrugs. "Girl, if you are pregnant, they will find out eventually when you come back to buy pampers and milk. So shut up! Pick a damn test."

I looked at the tests, but I was unsure of which one.

"Girl," Ebony said, "You need to be quicker with your decisions. You are about to be a whole mother. I, myself, will pop a Plan B pill first, and wait that shit out."

I groaned and grabbed the first one she picked out. I did need to make better decisions like use condoms.

Ebony raised an eyebrow. "Damn, just one?"

I glared at her. "I already took one."

She smirks, "Buy different ones for a second opinion. You want to be sure sure. How many other girls you think been to this same pharmacy because of him?"

I looked at Ebony and rolled my eyes. "Don't start!"

She grabbed two different tests, and I glared at her. I shrugged. She was right again about being sure.

She grabbed a third one for good measure.

I stared at her. Ebony didn't care.

"Look here, Fertile Myrtle, I am not taking any chances. We need hard proof."

She tossed a pack of Oreos into the basket as we walked by the snack aisle. "You gon' need comfort food either way, while we wait for the results."

I stare at her. "Can we just check out?"

She laughed, "Of course… Mommy."

I scowl at her. "Can you just pay for the tests?"

She handed me the basket as we walked to the register. "You pay for it. At this point, I am just here for emotional support."

So I pushed her out of the way…

Love Child...

I sat on my bed, staring at the last pregnancy test in my hand while Ebony ate my Oreos. She said she was stress eating. She ate all of them. Dammit.

Pink lines.

Pregnant.

One was positive with a plus sign.

Pregnant.

One was digital, no second-guessing.

Pregnant.

No squinting at faint lines or tilting it in the light. Clear, undeniable proof. Pregnant.

Ebony took it from me before I could even process what that meant.

She held it up like a coach about to give the victory speech of the century. Then stopped.

"Well... damn." She let out a low whistle. "What if it's twins or triplets? We need names!"

I groaned and buried my face in my hands.

"Ebony, please."

She wasn't even listening to me.

She turned the stick upside down, trying to see if the results would change.

"Girl, this test is bold as hell. Ain't no, maybe on here. This thing said, 'Pregnant.'" She almost sang the word.

I sighed. "What the hell am I supposed to do?"

Ebony plopped down beside me. "First, stop looking like somebody just handed you a prison sentence. This ain't the end of the world. This is my little niece, nephew, or both."

I lifted my head. "It's close enough."

She nudged my knee. "So… when are you telling Shawn? I want to beat his ass when you do."

I exhaled. "I don't know if I am. I will go to health services to see if they can set an appointment for me to be checked out by a doctor. Then, we will know what to do. Until then, we wait. We'll figure it out then."

Ebony gave me a sympathetic look. "Smart."

I took another deep breath and said, "I don't want to tell Shawn until I decide if I should even keep it."

Ebony's head snapped toward me so fast I thought she got whiplash. "I know you are lying. If? What did I tell you? I am right here, girl. You are not going to let how your Mom did you, or my Mom did me, change how we handle this. I told you, you got me. I am all in."

Ebony never really talked about the fact that her grandmother had to pick her up from the hospital after her mother left her there. Her grandmother shared it with me. Ebony must've heard us talking and joined us.

Ebony's mother has been on drugs, and the only time she saw her was to ask Ebony's grandmother for money. Ebony was smart. She knew.

Ebony never knew her father and never asked about him. Her mother is in a woman's prison in Pennsylvania. She never even went to visit her or wrote to her. Ebony didn't really talk about her life. Maybe that is why she poured all of this interest into my life.

Out of respect, I didn't ask. She became, who she needed most in her mother to me, a caregiver.

Here I was, selfishly putting this on her still.

"I am sorry for dropping this all on you, Ebony." I meant every word.

Ebony didn't say another word. She just hugged me.

I looked at her, my stomach twisting.

I was glad she was here.

I decided to change the subject to Shawn, and by Shawn, I meant Keisha.

"Keisha already got a sixth sense about me. If she finds out, she'll blow everything up."

Ebony waved her hand like she was swatting a fly.

"And? That's not your problem. Girl, let her blow something up. I'll bring the match."

I shot her a look. "That's not helping."

She twisted toward me on the bed, all jokes gone for a second. Ebony started again.

"NeeNee, listen to me. I know you are scared, but you don't get to make this decision based on some bitter broad who is probably sniffing around Shawn's phone as we speak. It's your choice as to when, and if, you do. This baby is not about her. Or you and Shawn now."

I chewed my lip. "What if he doesn't want it?"

Ebony shrugged. "Then he doesn't. But that doesn't change the fact that you are having it."

I didn't respond because I didn't know what I wanted or needed right now. Again, Ebony was right.

Ebony sighed and pulled me into a side hug. "You gon' be alright. You always are."

I leaned into her, just for a second, and then I sat back up. "What if I'm not?"

She pulled back and smacked my arm. "Then I'll be alright for you. Somebody gotta be for Baby Shawn Junior or Baby ShawnNeeNee. You know the twins. My nephew and my niece. Their parents are crazy."

That made me laugh.

"That name is ugly, too," I said.

Ebony looked at me and laughed, "I know."

Ebony looked at me again, and laughed louder.

"What?" I asked curiously.

"What about Shawnior, Shawn Junior? Ain't no need to be creative. ShawNeeQua! That baby is going to come out looking just like him. You do know babies snitch with their whole faces. It will be fine like his daddy."

I groaned, then laughed. "Damn, Ebony, stop playing."

Ebony laughed, "We are going to do things different. Besides, tradition isn't nothing but peer pressure from dead people. Don't do this. Don't say that. The way you should do it is. I didn't raise my children like that. Girl, if that baby comes out with an owner's manual, I will be the first to apologize and be wrong."

Then, I looked at the pregnancy tests again.

Deep down, I still wasn't sure if I was ready for what came next, but I had Ebony…

Nothing Even Matters…

After it spread all over campus, that Shawn "allegedly" proposed to Keisha, before I could get to health services, I decided not to tell Shawn.

The next day, Ebony and I saw Shawn and Keisha together, and we decided to do the one thing most people can't: We shut up. I wasn't ready.

Ebony didn't press me to tell either.

She was cool about it.

She finally got it.

We spent the next day figuring out how to handle the baby and stay in school.

"My grandmother, the saintly Mary Magdalene, will not be killing the both of us." Ebony joked.

If we put our checks together, we could get an apartment off campus. One of us goes to school in the day and the other at night. It could work.

Ebony said she needed weekends off to date.

Winter break came and went in a blur of morning sickness. After Christmas, which I spent with Ebony and her grandmother, I went back to school to work, trying to save more money with the baby.

Ebony's grandmother figured it all out, but only said she was happy for me. I tried to stay busy, my hands full, so my mind didn't have room to wander.

I wouldn't have to think about him. Shawn.
Shawn did call at least once a day in the beginning. He didn't understand my distance.

Then, when I didn't answer, the calls slowed down.

We had already stopped having sex.

A few brief texts would follow.

Are you good?

I wanna talk.

NeeNee and a heart.

I deleted every single one. I don't know why.

By the next week, the calls and texts stopped completely. I saw him. He looked miserable. I felt even bad about all this, but he had Keisha.

He chose her. But instead, there was this quiet, nagging emptiness sitting in my chest like a concrete brick. I missed him.

I told myself it was for the best.

This was his senior year.

He had other things to focus on.

And me? I needed to keep my head down, handle my business, and forget this happened. For Shawn's sake, not mine.

I had been doing good with the plan—until the second week of the spring semester.

That's when I realized forgetting Shawn would never be as easy as ignoring a few calls.

It started small.

I'd see him across the quad, standing in a circle of friends from the team. His voice carried over the breeze like a song I used to love but now couldn't stand to hear. So I walked away.

Where will you go, NeeNee?

Good question.

Then there were the close calls—ducking into hallways when I spotted him walking toward me, or pretending to be deep in conversation whenever I saw him.

I even started timing my shifts at the student center just right to avoid the hours I knew he'd be around with Keisha or his friends.

But my luck ran out on a random Tuesday.

I had just finished my shift. My feet were aching, and my body was running on fumes, when I heard him.

"NeeNee." My whole body stiffened

I could have kept walking.

I should have, but I didn't.

Instead, I turned around slowly, already trying to fight to keep from telling him everything, that I was pregnant, and that it was his.

Shawn stood a few feet away, hands in his pockets, studying me like he was trying to read my mind. I wouldn't let him. I couldn't let him.

"You got a minute?" His voice was more gentle than I expected. He was waiting to see if I would listen to him or walk away. So, no, I didn't have a minute.

Instead of saying that, I crossed my arms and asked, "What do you want?"

His face showed his confusion. "You are gonna act like I don't exist? Did Keisha say something?"

I looked past him, my pulse thumping. "I don't know what you're talking about."

He huffed a dry laugh. "NeeNee, you have been dodging me all this time. Come on. I am not stupid."

I shrugged. "I've been busy."

"That's the best you got?" He shook his head.

"You really are gon' act like nothing happened between us? Like we didn't mean something to each other?" His southern accent suddenly came on strong.

"There's nothing to talk about." I lied.

He took a step closer, and I stepped back.

133

His eyes darkened, frustration rolling off of him in waves. "NeeNee, stop playing. What happened?"

I knew I had to hurt him to make him stop. "You have a whole girlfriend. A fiancé. I heard. Go be with her."

"NeeNee—" Shawn said, reaching out to me.

I pulled away, and I started to walk off.

I didn't stop when he called my name again.

I wanted to.

I didn't even look back.

I just kept walking. I forced myself to breathe. I forced my feet to move, even though every part of me wanted to turn around. I wouldn't let myself do that.

If I did, what would I say to him that would make him even want to be with me, and not with Keisha, except for my baby, his baby, our baby...

Miss Me With That...

I kept my head down for the rest of the week, diving into schoolwork and shifting my schedule around to avoid any more run-ins with Shawn. But the universe had other plans. It was Friday night, and Ebony had to finally convince me to step out.

"Girl, if you don't get up and get dressed," she said from my doorway, hands on her hips, staring me down like a disapproving mother.

I groaned from my spot on my bed. "I don't feel like it. My body hurts. I feel like I am dying."

"Who is Diane?" Ebony asked with a snicker.

"Funny." I threw a pillow at her.

"You never feel like it, but guess what?" Ebony said, unbothered. "I'm not letting you rot away in this dorm like some sad-ass ghost of Christmas past. Put some damn clothes on."

I sighed. "Where are we even going?"

"Some party. I do not even know who is throwing it. I know it's where we need to be. All we do is work, sleep, and study. Okay, maybe you study."

Thirty minutes later, I found myself in the middle of a packed house party, music thumping through my bones, the air thick with sweat, liquor, and bad decisions. Then again, I wasn't drinking with Shawn.

Ebony was already in her element, flirting with a guy in the corner, leaving me alone to hover near the wall, clutching my soda like a lifeline. Then I felt it.

It was a shift in the air.

A presence that made my skin prickle.

I turned my head slightly—and my heart stopped.

Shawn. Yes, Shawn Shawn.

He was across the room, talking to some people, his body angled toward them, but his eyes?

His eyes were on me.

My stomach flipped.

I tore my gaze away, staring into my soda as if it had the answers to all of my problems.

I needed to leave right now.

I pushed off the wall, weaving through the crowd toward the door, but a hand caught my wrist before I could escape.

I already knew who it was before I even turned around. I didn't want to even look at him.

Shawn stood there before me, closer than he had been in months. His fingers burned against my skin, but he didn't let go.

"You are really about to do this? To run away from me at a party now?" His voice was low, rough.

"I'm not running," I lied. I was running.

His grip loosened, but he didn't step back. "Talk to me, NeeNee. Please talk to me."

"There's nothing to talk about."

His jaw clenched. "You keep saying that, but I don't believe you. What is going on with you?"

I swallowed hard, glancing around, hoping Ebony would swoop in and save me, but she was nowhere to be found. Dammit, Ebony.

Shawn exhaled, running a hand over his face before looking at me again, something sadder in his eyes now.

"Just tell me one thing." He said over the music.

I held my breath to hear what he had to say.

"Do you regret it? Is it the guilt that did this?"

My breath got caught in my chest.

I could've said no, and I told him everything.

I could've lied, said yes, and I walked away.

The words wouldn't come out.

I wanted to tell him that I didn't want to do what my mother did to my father and make him feel like he had to be with me because of a baby. I couldn't do that to him. Not to us.

I knew how that turned out. He knew about it.

And Shawn saw my hesitation. The truth was written all over my face. We made a mistake.

His eyes darkened. "Yeah. That's what I thought. It was me. I am the issue."

Before I could respond and figure out what I was even supposed to say, a voice cut through the tension.

"So this is why you have been acting weird?"

I turned—only to find Keisha standing a few feet away, her arms crossed, suspicion written all over her face. Shawn stiffened beside me.

My heart hammered in my chest.

Shit.

Not her again…

No More Drama...

Keisha's eyes bounced between Shawn and me, sharp and calculating, like a sniper.

She was dressed to be seen—a tight blue dress, heels clicking on the wooden floor, as she stepped closer, even over the music.

I felt the walls closing in. My breath caught in my throat. I didn't need this right now.

Shawn shifted beside me, his jaw tight. "Keisha, what are you talking about? I don't feel like this shit."

She huffed out a laugh, tilting her head. "Oh, now you wanna play dumb? And when will you be ready?"

Her gaze flicked towards me.

"No, something has not been adding up. You have been really weird for months, and now I see why."

She looked at me, but I felt like she was talking to Shawn. I felt trapped under the weight of her stare.

I forced a blank expression, even though my pulse was racing. "I don't know what you're talking about. I have nothing to do with that. Shawn is with you."

Keisha sucked her teeth, crossing her arms. "Of course, you don't. Play dumb just like he does!"

Her eyes never left mine, like she was waiting for me to crack under pressure.

Keisha continued, "It's just so convenient that somehow, NeeNee, Shawn always finds you, like he has your location. Like you're his pet project."

"I don't have time for your insecurities," I replied, but something in Shawn's eyes said that she was right.

Shawn always found me. I couldn't figure it out either.

I realized one thing about Keisha: in all of this, she was more afraid of losing Shawn than I was.

She was scared that I might be the only thing standing in the way of her happiness with him.

She was scared that I was not about to up and walk away from him.

And then, I saw it, as Keisha wiggled her fingers. Her engagement ring.

So, the rumors were true. They were engaged.

And if that wasn't enough, I finally tore my eyes away from her ring to hear what she was trying to say above the music and the noise.

Keisha said, "If I wasn't pregnant…"

You Don't Understand...

The words hung in the air like a slap in my face.

If she wasn't pregnant? And then what?

A slight grin crossed Keisha's face, as the words finally registered, and I looked at Shawn for his reaction.

Clearly, it was his. Who else would she have been sleeping with, and for how long?

Shawn's posture was tense, but his voice was smooth when he said, "Why the fuck did you tell her that?

Keisha smiled at him. "I was just so happy; I couldn't hold it in much longer. We're starting a family."

Shawn looked at me again. His eyes darted from Keisha to me and back again. He was upset that I had to find out like this. I, on the other hand, was devastated. Now I really couldn't tell Shawn. Nope.

"Congratulations," I said half-heartedly.

"That's why I wanted to clear up any misunderstandings before the big day," Keisha replied. Here she goes with the fake shit. "I want to know point blank, period, what is going on between you two. It's weird now. How he talks about you? I don't like it."

Her tone still sent a chill down my spine. She wasn't just throwing accusations around—she felt something. Woman's intuition, maybe? I didn't care at this point.

"It has been all of this weird energy between the two of you? It's been like this for a minute." She went on without missing a beat. "Well, now, that shit is over."

The fact that she noticed it was worse than anything she could have known. Is this how Shawn felt about me? He loves me, but still proposed to her out of obligation? He was doing it for the baby, despite me.

I needed to go. I wasn't ready for this.

"I have nothing to do with whatever's going on between y'all," I said, stepping back. "Shawn, handle that."

And now that she was pregnant, and had his engagement ring on her finger, she won.

I had to love him enough to let him go.

I turned to leave, but Keisha wasn't done.

"That's right," she muttered. "Run off like you always do. You got Shawn fooled, but not me."

I turned back around and Shawn stopped me.

I should've kept walking, should've let it slide. But something about how she said it—like she knew me and had the right to speak on me—sent heat rushing through my veins. I turned back, lifting my chin.

"And what's that supposed to mean?"

Keisha smirked. "I see you, NeeNee. You like to play quiet, play innocent, but you ain't fooling nobody. You were real comfortable standing next to my man just now. It was almost like you belonged there."

I laughed. "Shawn and I are just great friends."

Her smirk widened. "Then why do you look so guilty? I thought you two were just 'friends.'"

Keisha laughed, but there was no humor in it.

I was two seconds from saying something reckless, but then I caught the look on Shawn's face—warning me, silently begging me not to take the bait. She wasn't worth it and that he would check her for me.

I swallowed hard, forcing myself to take a deep breath.

Shawn stepped in, his voice firm. "Keisha! Shut up!"

"Oh, I'm chill. I think it's funny how some people don't know their place, Shawn. Train your pet."

Pet? I was over being nice. Through with how she was talking to me. This quiet girl. Let me take up space.

So, I said, "Keisha, if I wanted Shawn, you wouldn't be his ex. You'd be a memory he lied about. He would be fucking me right now. I'd be his stress relief, and you'd be the reason he needed it. You need a title. Now you are mad at me for what? You are keeping tabs on me. If you're scared call the cops. You won, miss."

And Shawn, it was like he saw me for the first time...

I'm Gonna Be Alright...

Did I see a smile curl at Shawn's lips? I did.

Keisha, though, she looked like I slapped her.

"Shawn," she shrieked. "Are you going to let her talk to me like that. She was so terrible to me. See!"

Shawn looked me. "You started it. She finished it."

This wasn't my fight though. She was fighting her own insecurities and projecting them onto me. I had already done enough damage. My baby didn't need this stress.

"Whatever, you dumb bitch," I said, turning and pushing through the crowd. I left. I didn't run.

I didn't stop until I was outside, the night air hitting my skin like a slap. I gulped it down, my heart still racing.

Someone was behind me.

"Damn, girl," Ebony's voice came from my left. "What just happened? Why are you out here?"

I nearly jumped. "Where have you been?"

She sipped from her cup, giving me a lazy grin. "Minding my business and getting some numbers. But clearly, you have been busy."

I rolled my eyes. "It's nothing."

Ebony side-eyed me. "NeeNee, do I look stupid? I just saw Shawn and Keisha. She is mad as fuck."

I sighed, running a hand through my hair. "Keisha is pregnant, and based on the ring on her finger, they are engaged."

Ebony's eyes widened, and then she grinned. "Ooooh, so the rumor is true. Lucky bitch."

"This isn't funny, Ebony." I replied.

She bit her lip, trying to hold back a laugh. "Girl, it's a little funny. I was going to kill her if we needed to get her out of the way. I saw the show, and I can get away with it. All I need is trophy to hit her with."

"Now, I am glad I didn't tell Shawn. It would have only complicated his life more. It is really over." I remarked.

Ebony looked at me with sympathy, "Or it would have made him choose you, once and for all."

I groaned. "I need to go get in my bed. I am tired."

Ebony looped her arm through mine.

"Fine, fine. But you will tell me everything on the way. It's funny how she is pregnant now. You were about to be a co-mama with a chick that looks like she spells 'congratulations' with a 'd.'" Ebony said.

I laughed and let her pull me towards our dorm, but as we walked away, I felt it—eyes on me.

I turned slightly.

Shawn was standing nearby, watching me go, with a confused expression. I knew he wanted to say something. He was mad at how she handled that whole thing. It was all over his face. That was on them.

And Keisha? What kind of name is Keisha?

She was standing not far from him, her eyes narrowed, lips curled in a knowing look.

You could see it in her eyes. She was upset.

I looked away, my stomach twisting.

She won… for now.

Ebony was right, though; it is funny how conveniently she is pregnant now.

Ebony turned back to look at Shawn. I heard him yell.

I thought Ebony was mouthing to him that she was going to fuck him up. Instead, she was watching Shawn and Keisha go at it verbally. They were fighting.

Ebony stopped in her tracks as we both watched them arguing. "Cuss that bitch out, Shawn," she yelled.

I had never seen Shawn like that. Not with me.

He was upset with her. See that Aries man.

Just then, Keisha reached for Shawn's arm, but he snatched it away and walked off…

A Song For Mama...

I stood in front of my bathroom mirror, staring at the undeniable curve of my stomach. My hands rested against it, fingers lightly tracing the shape of the life growing inside me.

There was no hiding it anymore.

The big hoodies and oversized sweatpants weren't fooling anyone—not Ebony, not the nosy ladies in the dining hall where I worked, and would not fool him, if he saw me. The weather was getting too warm for that.

I had spent the last few days dodging his frequent calls and his pop ups, convincing myself that keeping this secret was for the best. But now, there was no escaping it. It showed in my face. I gained weight.

My phone buzzed on the desk.

I hesitated before picking it up, my heart pounding as I saw his name flash across the screen. Shawn Jonathan Conquest and his picture.

I swallowed hard, then answered. "Hello?"

For a second, there was only silence. Then, his voice—soft, unsure. "NeeNee?"

I haven't talked to him since the party, but the whole campus knew about him and Keisha, and how they had that huge fight afterwards.

I heard him say my name. Hearing him say my name sent a familiar warmth through me, but I pushed it aside. Instead I just said, "Hey."

He let out a breath. "Damn, NeeNee, finally. I—I don't even know where to start."

He sounded frantic almost. I stayed quiet.

"Look," he continued. "I know you've been avoiding me, and I know I should've tried harder to talk to you. But… I wanted to tell you. I only asked her to marry me out of obligation for her and the baby. I apologize."

"I understand," I said, even though I didn't.

"I thought it was the right thing to do," he said, voice tight. "And I was trying to keep it from hurting you."

"I am fine." I lied again. "I want you to be happy."

"I would never do anything to hurt you." His tone was raw, like the weight of those words still sat heavy on his chest. "I didn't mean for this to get this far."

Curiously, I asked, "So now what?"

"I don't know," Shawn said, sounding defeated.

I pressed a hand to my stomach.

Keisha is pregnant.

And here I was, carrying his baby and he doesn't know. All of this time, I thought about what he needed. I forgot about what I needed. What about my baby and my baby's future? I still have a year left of school.

"NeeNee, are you still there?" I heard Shawn ask.

I opened my mouth, but nothing came out.

"I need to see you," he said, more urgent this time. "Please. Even if it is for a few minutes."

I closed my eyes. There was no more running.

No more hiding.

"Okay," I said. "I have something that I need to tell you though. Why I have been acting weird towards you. I don't want you to be angry with me. I didn't know how to tell you. I have been trying to for weeks now."

"NeeNee, there is nothing that you can say that will make me change how I feel about you?" He paused. "NeeNee, I love you. I always will."

"I love you too," I said, then I took a deep breath and said the quiet part out loud, "And I'm pregnant..."

Made For Me...

I sat on the front steps of my dorm, arms wrapped around my stomach, dreaming, as I waited for Shawn.

I was trying to figure out what I wanted to say to him. I had to explain everything to him. I decided to just show him my stomach. Let him see things for himself.

He had a right to know why I did this.

The night air was cool, wrapping around me in soft waves. I replayed our conversation a little while ago in my head. He wasn't upset when I said the words.

He had sounded different—worn down, tired when he told me about Keisha. But when I said I was pregnant, he sounded genuinely happy, and even, upbeat.

I didn't want him upset when the initial shock wore off and he had time to think. My stomach fluttered as I thought about how this might change everything.

I had to check myself a couple of times to make sure I wasn't dreaming. I did that, sometimes, I fantasized.

We agreed on a time, and I was patiently waiting, ready to talk to him finally. He just had one thing to do.

And if he chose not to stay and even help me and the baby, then I was okay with that, too...

Everything Comes To The Light...

I was about to go back in for a minute when I heard somebody call out my name.

It was Shawn.

His gaze locked on me instantly, taking me in like he hadn't seen me in years.

And then—his eyes dropped to my stomach.

Everything else faded.

The noise, the campus, the world.

He stepped forward, breath-catching.

"NeeNee..."

I stood slowly, letting my hands drop to my sides. I wanted him to see my stomach.

"I was going to tell you," I said quietly. "I just..."

His eyes met mine.

"It's mine, though?" Shawn asked tearfully.

I nodded, heart hammering in my chest, as if it was beating so hard, trying to get out.

Shawn ran a hand through his hair, staring at me like he was trying to process a million thoughts all at once.

Then—slowly, cautiously—he stepped closer and placed his hands on my stomach carefully.

A small, breathless laugh left his lips.

"I can't believe this," he whispered.

Then he looked up at me, his eyes shining.

"You're having my baby?" He said.

I swallowed past the lump in my throat.

"Yeah." I whispered back.

And then, before I could say anything else, he pulled me into his arms, holding me like he never wanted to let go.

A wave of emotion crashed over me—relief, fear, joy.

But above all?

Love.

I don't know.

This wasn't what I had planned.

For the first time in a long time, though, it felt right.

I felt safe in his arms again.

"I want to be here," he murmured against my hair as he held me.

"I don't care what it takes. I want this. I want you." I heard him say.

I clutched his shirt, breathing him in. "Me too."

His hands cupped my face, tilting my head up so that I had no choice but to see the truth in his eyes. "I'm all in, NeeNee. I will handle Keisha."

I nodded, a smile tugging at my lips. "Me too."

He grinned, his thumb brushing my cheek.

"Come on. Let's go somewhere and talk."

I agreed and asked where he parked his car.

As he walked away, I exhaled, pressing my hands to my stomach.

Everything was about to change.

For the first time in months, I wasn't scared.

I was happy.

I allowed myself to be happy for the first time in a long time.

Keisha was no longer standing in my way.

I stopped and spun around.

Screamed out "yes" to nobody in particular.

Shawn looked at me and laughed.

I looked up, and Ebony was yelling out of the window.

"It's about damn time, you two."

But I would be lying to you, myself, and God, if I said that is what happened.

I don't even remember everything that happened.

I remember walking across the campus to the parking lot.

I saw Shawn's car.

Then, I decided to walk to him and talk to him.

As I stepped into the street, I saw headlights coming at me. A car was swerving. Driving all crazy.

Then I knew how a deer might have felt...

NeeNee's Accident... Junior Year

Thump. Thump.

I never saw the car coming.

Thump. Thump.

I promise you I didn't.

Thump. Thump.

One minute, my mind was racing with things I wanted to say to Shawn, and then, the next...

Blinding headlights.

Thump. Thump.

Screeching tires.

Thump. Thump.

Somebody was driving like they were drunk.

Thump. Thump.

And then—impact.

Thump. Thump.

And then, the sound of a car speeding away.

They didn't even stop to see if they killed me.

Thump. Thump.

If I was dead.

Thump. Thump.

I thought I was hearing the sounds of some drums, but that was the sound of my heartbeat and the pain that rocked my body.

Thump. Thump.

Pain that had exploded through me as I was thrown into the air.

I was weightless for a terrifying second before crashing down hard to the ground, like a human rag doll would.

The world tilted, the sky spinning above me as shouts and screams filled the air.

My ears rang, and my body refused to move; the sharp, metallic taste of blood filled my mouth. It was my blood.

I gasped for breath and I was forced to swallow more.

My hands instinctively went to my stomach.

Wait! My baby!

Was it too late to protect it?

No!

Through the chaos, I heard Shawn's voice.

Panicked.

Broken.

Scared.

Footsteps pounded against the pavement as others gathered around me, and then, he slid to his knees, beside me.

"NeeNee, stay with me, okay?

His hands hovered over me, shaking.

"Somebody call an ambulance," he yelled.

I tried to speak, but the pain stole my words.

Tears blurred my vision as my hands gripped his.

At least he is here.

Please, God!

Could you not take this away from me, too!

Shawn cupped my face, his own eyes wet with tears.

"Stay with me, baby, please!"

Darkness crept at the edges of my vision, but I fought against it, trying to focus on his face.

I tried to focus on the life growing inside of me.

I heard Shawn scream, "She is pregnant!"

Thump. Thump.

I let out a scream.

Thump. Thump.

And then, everything went black…

Lucid Dreams...

Pain. That's all I felt. Unbearable pain.

That was the first thing I felt.

It ripped through me, hot and sharp, like someone had set fire to every nerve in my body.

I never felt anything like it before.

My head pounded, my limbs felt heavy, and for a moment, I didn't know where I was.

Then, I heard a voice—desperate, breaking.

"NeeNee, I'm right here."

It was Shawn. Was this real or a dream?

I fought against the darkness pulling at me, forcing my eyes open. It was him and Ebony. Or was it?

"Girl, you had us worried," Ebony said.

The light above me was blinding. Everything around me was a blur. As my vision adjusted, I saw them.

Shawn was hovering over me, his face pale, his eyes red-rimmed. Ebony said that he never left my side. One of them had to be sitting beside my bed when I woke up. A sense of calm washed over me.

His hands gripped mine so tightly, it was like he was scared I'd slip away if he let go.

Relief crashed over him the second our eyes met. And Ebony wouldn't stop crying.

Ebony said her grandmother never stopped praying when she found out. Ebony went to call her.

"Oh, thank God," he whispered, his voice thick. "Good, you're finally awake."

I tried to speak, but my throat was raw, and all that came out was a weak croak. The pain got me.

"Don't talk, Ni---," he said quickly, squeezing my hand. "You're in the hospital. Don't worry; they caught the person who did this, who tried to hit you and drive off like a maniac."

Was it Keisha?

I know that's what you were thinking. I was.

That she wanted to kill me.

Memories slammed into me all at once.

The headlights. The impact. The pain.

My stomach.

My baby.

I tried to move, panic seizing my chest, but Shawn held me still.

"Don't move too much," Shawn said.

His voice wavered, and I noticed the tears on his face for the first time. "You scared the hell out of me, Ni---."

I swallowed hard, trying to steady my breathing. Then, my hand instinctively went to my stomach as Ebony returned to the room. Shawn sucked in a sharp breath.

"Shawn," I croaked. My voice barely audible, but I didn't care. "The baby…?"

His grip on my hand tightened. My head throbbed.

Terror gripped me as his eyes glossed over again. "Shawn—"

"The baby's okay," he whispered, his voice was filled with emotion. Ebony's eyes said otherwise. She looked away from me. What was going on? I'm confused.

"You almost lost it, NeeNee. But the doctors… they saved the baby." Shawn said.

A sob ripped from my throat as relief washed over me so hard I thought I might pass out again. Thankfully, I didn't. I should be awake. I didn't want to sleep.

Shawn exhaled shakily and leaned forward, pressing his forehead against my hand.

"I thought I lost you," he whispered.

"I thought I lost both of you."

Tears slipped down my face as I let the weight of everything sink in.

I am alive.

My baby is alive.

I closed my eyes for a second, trying to gather my thoughts, and when I opened them again, Shawn was already staring at me. His expression had changed to sadness. He was staring at me. It was… different.

"This has changed everything," he murmured.

I blinked. "What does?"

His jaw tightened. "I'm not leaving you again, NeeNee. I won't let you go."

His voice was filled with something I wasn't used to hearing from him—confusion.

"You and this baby—" His hand went to my stomach. "Our baby! I'm not going anywhere."

Tears burned my eyes. "Shawn…"

"I mean it." His voice was firm. "I should've fought harder for you. I should've made you talk to me sooner. But I'm here now, and I'm not leaving. We need to be together. Keisha is gone. We are through. I told her."

I searched his face, my heart hammering.

He looked serious.

More determined.

Unshakable.

I had spent months running from this.

From him.

But now, lying in this hospital bed, realizing just how close I had come to losing everything… I couldn't run anymore. I didn't want to.

None of this was making sense though.

Shawn's fingers brushed my cheek, his touch gentle and reverent. "I love you, Ni---."

I swallowed hard, then said. "I love you, Sugar Bear."

His lips curved into a small, relieved smile. "Good. That's the way it should always be."

Then, his expression hardened. "Because after what just happened? I'm not taking any more chances. Not ever again."

I frowned. "What do you mean?"

He exhaled and leaned in, his face inches from mine.

"I'm gonna take care of you," he whispered. "You and our baby. I don't care. I'm gonna make this right."

As I lay there, my fingers brushing my stomach, one thought echoed in my mind.

A shiver ran through me as Ebony laughed.

Wait, I thought Ebony went to call her grandmother.

For the first time...I believed him. This felt different, though. Then, Ebony was suddenly gone.

It was just me and him in the dorm.

Something is not right, but what?

I am so confused.

Wait! Did I make all of this up in my head.

Shawn never calls me Ni---!

What is going on?

I wanted to scream for Ebony!

Then Shawn was gone.

I was alone.

I closed my eyes and tried to wake myself.

I turned and I was back in that street.

Blinded by the lights from the car that hit me.

Thump. Thump.

Then the car hit me again. Then again.

It was only then that I woke up for real...

Never Been To Me...

The first thing I noticed when I finally woke up was the silence. Nothing but silence. I learned to hate quiet.

No machines beeping. No doctors hovering over me.

Just the steady hum of something distant, like the world had muffled itself just for me. It was just too quiet.

I blinked up at the bright hospital ceiling, my throat dry, my body aching in places I couldn't even name.

I hurt hurt. That was the way I honestly felt.

My fingers curled against the rough hospital sheets as the memories started flooding back—the accident, the headlights, and at least, my baby was safe.

My stomach clenched, as if on cue.

I reached down instinctively, my trembling hand pressing against my belly.

Something felt... wrong.

My stomach felt... flat.

Empty.

The room spun as reality slammed into me like a wrecking ball.

No! No, no, no, no, no—

The door opened, and before I could force a sound past the lump in my throat, Shawn was there, his face tired, his eyes filled with something I couldn't read.

I struggled to sit up, my heart pounding so hard it made my head throb.

"Shawn," my voice came out raspy.

"Where's—" I tried again after clearing my throat. It sounded just as bad as before.

Tears welled in his eyes before I even finished the question. That was all it took.

I shook my head violently. "No!"

My voice was hoarse, barely above a whisper.

"No, tell me it's not true." He didn't answer.

"Shawn."

My voice cracked. Panic rose in my chest.

"Tell me!"

His face crumpled as he sat on the edge of the bed, reaching for me. "NeeNee, I—"

I smacked his hand away so fast that I barely registered the sting in my palm.

"Don't touch me."

His mouth parted, but I didn't want to hear whatever he was about to say.

"I lost my baby!?" My voice was shaking so badly that I barely recognized it. "Where is my baby?"

Shawn's silence was the only answer I needed.

A sound I didn't even know I was capable of making ripped from my chest—a strangled, broken sob that shattered the silence in the room. They must have heard me in the halls. I didn't care. Let them hear me.

My body folded forward, my arms wrapping around my stomach, as if I could, somehow, put my baby back where it belonged.

Shawn tried to touch me again, but I shoved him back.

Was this real? Was I dreaming? This was very real.

"No! I want my baby!"

"NeeNee, please—"

"You told me—" My voice trembled with anger, grief, and devastation, all at once. "You told me everything was okay! You said we were fine! You lied to me!"

His face twisted with pain and confusion.

"NeeNee, this is the first time you woke up."

Then, reality really sat in. What was real? What was a dream? Did I just overhear them talking? What?

Suddenly, Ebony burst into the room. Then a nurse came, who was about to ask Shawn to leave, but Ebony gave her a dirty look. I know that's right.

"I wanted to be here to tell you when you were strong enough to know…" Shawn tried to say the words, but they didn't come out. There is nothing he could say.

"Oh, so you wanted to wait until I was strong enough to hear that my baby was gone? And then what?"

My voice was dripping with venom now.

"You wanted to break the news gently to me?" I asked.

Shawn dragged a hand down his face, exhaling shakily. "I just—I didn't want to break you the way it already broke me, NeeNee, when I found out."

"Well, congratulations." I let out a bitter laugh that felt more like a sob. "You failed. I'm broken."

Tears streamed down his face as he sat in front of me.

"NeeNee, I know you're hurting. But don't--"

"Don't." My voice dropped to a whisper. "Don't you dare act like you know how I feel? That was my baby."

Shawn flinched. He looked even more, if possible, hurt.

Wait, why did I say that? Hurt people hurt people.

No, I shouldn't have said that. Shawn stood up.

I turned away from him, staring out the window, willing myself to feel anything other than this crushing emptiness. This was my chance to have a family.

Shawn stood there for a long time, the silence stretching between us like an uncrossable canyon.

I could only think about my baby.

I didn't care about him. At least, not right now.

Then, finally, he spoke.

My eyes squeezed shut.

"I love you. We can get through this, NeeNee," he whispered. "Together. I swear to you; we can have more—" Wasn't he with that bitch, Keisha?

I snapped my head toward him. Something dark and raw was clawing its way up my throat. "More?"

He swallowed hard realizing what he just said.

"You think I can just replace my baby like it's nothing? Can I have another one and forget it? You go do that with Keisha. Isn't that your fiancé? Isn't she pregnant?"

Shawn tried to interject. "That's not what I meant—"

"Get out!" I replied.

His face paled. "NeeNee—"

"Get. Out." I said through clenched teeth.

The words came out cold. Emotionless. Shawn stared at me, his chest rising and falling like he was trying to breathe through the pain, and nothing in him was strong enough. He felt every word.

"I am not giving up on you," he said quietly.

I turned away from him again. "You already lost me. You lost me. Go back to Keisha."

I didn't say another word. What could I say?

I just sat there, staring out at the sky, as the weight of my loss crushed me completely. Ebony sat down next to me. The nurse checked my vitals and left after Shawn did. She patted my leg on the way out.

Ebony looked at me and quietly said, "NeeNee, I love you, but that was wrong. They caught the one who hit you. He was high as a damn kite. Not Shawn. Shawn didn't cause this, and he shouldn't have to apologize to you for it. You owe him an apology."

"But Ebony..." I started to say.

"No," Ebony took a deep breath and spoke again. "He has been here day and night. If I had somebody in my life like that, I wouldn't let go. He didn't know you were even pregnant until when? He is hurting right now and you didn't even ask if he was okay? If I was okay? I still love you and I get it. Does he? This is Shawn. You even say his name twice like Shawn Shawn because he has been your heart since you met him. You're wrong..."

I Let You Walk Away...

The rest of the semester came and went in a blur of forced normalcy. I tried to make it that way.

I worked on campus as usual, stayed in my dorm most of the time with Ebony hovering, and avoided Shawn as if my life depended on it. And the sympathy stares.

Shawn reminded me of the pain that I felt when I thought of him and our baby. It wasn't his fault.

Ebony was right.

I hurt him, and he didn't deserve any of that.

So I eventually called him to apologize, but he let it go to voicemail. I left countless messages. I felt stupid.

I tried from different numbers. He knew I hated answering strange numbers. That's like picking up a hitchhiker. When I went to his dorm, he wasn't there.

I saw him once across campus, but he was gone before I could talk to him. He looked tired. I did that to him.

I felt even worse. He didn't deserve anything that I did to him. Ebony saw me and told me to let him be.

I owed him that. I broke him. He lost our baby as well, not just me, and I wasn't there to support him.

He was graduating soon. That was the only good thing about all of this. Because once he was gone, we could all move on. I saw that Ebony missed him, too. She just didn't let on. She was better than me. I still was hurting.

On the day of his graduation, I saw him again.

I was all set to walk up to him and apologize when I saw him with a good group of people, so I walked away. It's his big day. Let him be. But he must have seen me.

He ran up to me in his cap and gown and gently reached for me. He probably thought I would pull away. I didn't hate him; I loved him, and I still love him.

Then, he looked back at the group, including a well-dressed man and woman who smiled at us. I realized this was his family. They gathered to watch us, probably with a million questions about who I am.

Shawn smiled like he had not smiled in days, and I felt a relief wash over me. I hope it was genuine.

"Congratulations, Mr. Conquest." I said cheerfully.

"You see me," Shawn smiled again. He was happy to see me. "Thank you. You helped to get me here. That is my family, if you want to meet them, to join us for lunch. Your choice. You can meet my Mom and Dad."

I shook my head no. "No. Thank you."

I paused, trying to gather my thoughts. "Shawn, what I want to say is that I am sorry. I apologize... for everything. I really want you to be happy now."

He nodded and said, "No, I should apologize to you for my part in all of this. We don't need to... I get it. I understand. Right now, I'm just glad I saw you before I left. To say goodbye. I want you to be happy too."

He smiled, but I could see the sadness in his eyes. He looked back at his family, who had started walking away to give us privacy. Had he told them about us? About me? The baby? I didn't care if he did.

"I have to go, but if you ever need me, my number won't change." Shawn looked for his family again and started walking away, still watching me. So, I turned to walk away. Then I heard Shawn call my name… "NeeNee!"

I turned around. He was still there. Watching me.

He then ran back over to me and kissed me with an intensity I had never felt. It took my breath away. He hugged me again briefly before taking a bunch of steps backwards, still watching me, as he moved away.

"If you ever stop running," he called out, "I will be right here, waiting for you! I love you, NeeNee! I love you!"

He turned and disappeared into the crowd. That was the last time I saw him. He was gone. And I felt it again. Alone. Lost. Confused. Scared. Sad. Broken. I was used to it. But never around him. Or with him.

I don't think people understand that some pain will kill every part of the person that you used to be. That's why there are no second chances in this life.

For it to work, a person would have to get to know you again. Most people don't. I would never be happy, and he deserved better than what I could give him. My question, what was I going to do now without him…

You Are My Friend...

You might call me stupid right now. I let him walk away. That I should have gone after him. I don't know how to fight. So go right ahead. I deserve it. I'm used to it.

Ebony avoided talking about Shawn until later that day when I helped her pack her stuff to return home. I told her that I had seen him and that we had talked briefly.

Ebony already knew about Shawn somehow. She told me Shawn already had a job in Atlanta working with his father. She claimed she only ear hustled about him because she cared about me. Even though she was friends with Shawn, she avoided him for me.

That's what real friends do. One band, one sound.

I had been so selfish in all of this. I forgot about Ebony's feelings. I never considered that she also lost Shawn and the baby. I never even meddled in her life.

And I became a good liar when it came to my life. I told myself it didn't matter that he was gone. I said it was better this way. I was finally free. It wasn't. I wasn't.

The hollow ache in my chest told a different story. This would be the love of my life. I might be crazy, but when I first mentioned his name, I thought I saw hope in her eyes for a brief second. Then, when I said Shawn had said goodbye, it was gone just as quickly. She knew.

For once, she didn't press the issue. This thing had changed all of us, and not for the better. Ebony and I didn't talk about the baby. There was nothing to say.

I did get counseling. I felt better that I did. It is okay to get help and talk to somebody. I needed that.

After we loaded everything in her car, Ebony looked at me like she didn't want to leave without me. I looked at her and said, "I'm a big girl now." I just prayed her car, with its rusty bottom, would get her to Brooklyn safely.

Her grandmother said I was more than welcome to stay with them. I lied that I was okay. I had arranged to stay on campus again for the summer. I needed the money.

Ebony hugged me tightly, promised to call me, and left, reminding me that she and her old beat-up Buick were just a phone call away. I almost cried. It hurt.

First, Shawn, and now Ebony was gone. That night, I lay in my dorm room and thought about everything I had been through. I cried like a baby for the first time since I used to do at Aunt Shirley's a lifetime ago.

And Keisha, she must have got what she wanted because she dropped out of school. I guess to follow Shawn back to Atlanta with their baby coming.

I thought about my mother and my father, and wherever they are, I hope they are happy. They made everything about them. People don't realize that when you have children, it is no longer about you. That child never asked to come into this world.

I touched my stomach and thought about my baby. I didn't even want to know if it was a boy or a girl. Shawn didn't know. I didn't want to know. I left the keepsake box the hospital gave me at the hospital unopened.

I was alone in the world again; maybe that was where I needed to be.

That night, I was about to go get something to eat when I saw a familiar face walking across the campus.

I screamed.

No, it wasn't Shawn. He left. He was gone.

It was Ebony.

I wondered why Ebony had not called me to say that she had made it back to Brooklyn safely. I was tempted to call her, but I leaned on her too much already.

Ebony and me, like something out of the ending the movie, "The Color Purple," we ran towards each other like Celie and Nettie. Ebony looked at me and hugged me as I cried. I cried like a baby. We both cried.

"Girl, I was near Philly when I called my nana and told her that I was turning back around. She told me to take care of your sister. So, I am right where I need to be."

"You came back for me?" I asked still crying.

Ebony smiled and said, "Nothing but death could keep me from it." And she hugged me and somehow everything that might have been broken, felt like it had been put back together again...

Michael Johnson… Senior Year

Then Michael showed up. Michael Johnson. Him.

I met Michael in my senior year of college, the fall semester, when graduation was coming too slowly, and I needed a job. It was back when I still wanted to believe in happy endings, despite the years my mother told me, growing up, that men ain't shit. Some weren't.

Before, I learned that love wasn't always enough, and before, I realized that some men could hold you close while their hearts were stretched thin between you and somebody else. And Shawn, I still never called him. I prayed he was happy, working, or something.

I wasn't even looking for Michael the first time I saw him. He had graduated a few years before I stepped on campus. After Shawn, I didn't want to know him.

Another campus legend from Long Island. Captain of this and that. Student government blah blah. He looked like he had a passport and traveled frequently, yet he found me. A broke girl from Philly. NeeNee.

It was one of those humid nights in D.C., where the heat clung to your skin like a bad memory. I would rather be in my bed reading. I needed a good book.

It was an "alumni event" during homecoming weekend that Ebony dragged me to. I told you she could talk the devil into anything. It was packed; the music was thumping, with one of Rihanna's songs so hard it shook the walls. I didn't want to be in here. I needed to study.

The smell of Hennessy and cheap weed tangled in the air, mixing with sweat, perfume, and cologne, and the promise of a better future, new fake friends, a fear of the future, and sheer desperation. I hated it.

I was standing there bored out of my mind, ready to go, when he walked in. He looked like something God took his time with and exuded confidence that made people step aside when he passed by. This was a grown man.

Ebony was already two shots deep, standing next to me with another dress that clung to her 5'4 thick frame. If she didn't work in a clothing store, I'd think Ebony should have been a stylist. She knew how to dress.

"Girl," she yelled over the music, "if you don't loosen up and stop standing there like you are somebody's chaperone, or an old woman's care nurse, I swear to God—" She said "God" like "Gawd." I laughed.

"I'm here," I replied, "Ain't I?"

"Yeah," she said with a look only Ebony can give, "But are you with me? Or are you up in that head of yours, thinking about shit you can't change? We are graduating this year! We are about to be broke broke."

I rolled my eyes and started thinking about Shawn. Mr. Popularity was always in the mix. He loved parties like this. I felt like he would walk through the door at any minute, surveying his kingdom, but since we got there, he didn't. "I told you I wasn't feeling this."

Ebony laughed, "You are a bad liar and didn't have a choice. You gotta live."

She wasn't wrong. Instead, I said, "I live." I lied.

Ebony laughed. "You live through school. That does not count. Since I met you, that's all you have done: work and go to school. I can't be your best friend if you will be boring. That would hurt my reputation."

She talked like the last year, or so, with Shawn, never happened. I needed that. I had been carrying the weight of my past around like an overstuffed suitcase for years. I needed to unpack that baggage too.

"Whatever." I finally said.

Before I could protest, Ebony was already dragging me through the event, which, in my opinion, meant a bunch of grown men in button-ups pretending to relive their college days, while the broke-ass seniors looked for future job connections. I didn't care.

I wasn't here for any of it until I saw him. And then, at that moment, my life changed. Not for the better.

And when I saw him, I almost felt trapped. His eyes were on me, heavy and steady, like he had already made up his mind about loving me. He won. I lost.

He was leaning against the wall, sipping a drink, taking his time studying me like I was an open-book test, and answering every question like he already knew who I was. I could feel the weight of his stares.

I turned to say something to Ebony, but she was already on the dance floor with some guy, allowing this man to speak to me. He moved slowly as he walked up to me like he had all the time in the world. Like he was unbothered by the chaos all around him.

"You keep looking at me like that; I might think you want something," he said smoothly.

"Boy, please," I replied, "I was trying to decide if you were really cocky, or just delusional."

He laughed. It wasn't that damn funny.

I should have played it cool.

I should have made him work for what we both wanted. And the way he looked at me? Like I was the most interesting thing in the room. I wasn't.

But I melted right there.

His smile widened, "I am the real thing, sweetheart."

That night, he took me to a spot he knew near campus. We walked, so we could talk. We talked until the place closed. He made me laugh. So, not all college men were overgrown boys just looking to score.

He made me feel safe. He made me forget for a while that I spent my whole life trying to prove I was worth staying for. The rest of the night was a blur of conversation and stolen glances. I wanted him.

Michael was smooth, but not in the forced, player way. You could tell he had manners and shit. I was right when I later checked him out. He was in law school and about to graduate. Good family. That was important.

He was attentive and leaned in when I spoke, asking me real questions as if he wanted to know me. I was like, Shawn, who? Michael wasn't just trying to freak me, either. If anything, he was a perfect gentleman.

When the night ended, he only asked for my number. I found myself saying yes. He was a nice guy at first. And just like that, I made my first mistake, of so many.

And not just about him. I wanted to be loved so badly that I forgot to check who might be doing it. That night when I told Ebony I let him walk me to what she called "the second location." The secluded spot he could have done whatever to me, she was heated at first.

Stranger danger she called it. Then, she googled him. She checked his social media. Verified his phone number. Just being protective. She was impressed.

He was everything some people only pretended to be.

So why was this all a mistake. See you were so caught up in Shawn, you didn't even realize I still had not met Michael's mother yet. I soon learned it wasn't Michael; who felt he wanted a wife. He needed me. But why?

The only problem is his mother didn't want just anybody around her son. My question was why? Maybe I read the situation wrong, but… you tell me.

Get comfortable…

When You Believe In Love…

Michael had me believing in love again. For the rest of my senior year, he drove down to D.C. on the weekends, or I would take the trip to New York. I stopped thinking about Shawn. Okay, I'm lying. I tried.

I did, but now and then when something Shawn said popped into my head, it was hard not to. I forgot about the time when Shawn and I first became friends, he practically begged me and Ebony to show him around New York. So, I gave in and we all went one weekend.

Shawn knew I used to live in New York and that Ebony was from Brooklyn. Being from Atlanta, Shawn had never been, and Shawn suggested we go to visit. Shawn loved it. I mean, he wanted to see everything.

I remembered when Shawn said jokingly, "I heard you ain't a real New Yorker until you've cussed out a cab driver, argued with a pigeon, and dodged a rat the size of a small puppy, all before breakfast."

He was a kid in a candy store in the city. I laughed the first time, and every time I thought about it. But I couldn't explain it to Michael. He didn't know Shawn.

He wouldn't get that kind of humor.

Ebony did. She was the one that brought it up.

She always brought up Shawn first.

During our first visit to Times Square, Shawn loved all of the sights and sounds. Best of all, Ebony's grandmother loved him. He threatened to eat her out of the house and home, too. She was ready for him, though. She made him a feast that weekend.

Michael. He took me to all of these fancy, expensive places in the city. He introduced me to many new things, such as the boring ass opera and his places with menus that didn't have a price. Galleries.

Not to meet his family though.

Not even during the holidays.

That should have been my red flag.

He said he wasn't ready. I wondered why, and then I remembered Shawn wanted to introduce me to his. It was wrong to compare him to Shawn. I shouldn't have done that. It wasn't fair to Michael or Shawn. But...

Shawn opened up to me while Michael was guarded. This was why I used to get so upset when he disappeared and I couldn't call them to check in on him.

When I graduated, I fell in love with the city so much that Ebony made sure we found jobs in the city. I found a job in marketing, as a publicist. I worked on a team.

It started out as a paid internship, but I treated it like school and worked my ass off to secure a better position. I needed that. I got it after just six months.

Ebony took a job as a science teacher. Yes, Ebony is smart, too. Look how she kept track of everything around her and me. She told me she wasn't going anywhere that I didn't follow. I knew it would bring her closer to her grandmother, so the deal was made.

It was Ebony's idea to move in together until one of us hopefully got married or shacked up. Her grandmother had even found a little "friend" of her own and was out being "fresh." Ebony kept telling her she wasn't grown. I told you Ebony is everyone's mother these days.

We spent some Sundays with Ms. Mary and her "friend," as she called him. It gave me a sense of family.

Michael was okay with me staying with Ebony. He often worked late, or was traveling. My job afforded me my own place, but I didn't mind at all. He said he felt better knowing Ebony was keeping me company.

Lately, it made me realize it gave him the freedom to do his own thing. Maybe that was it. I was in a relationship, he was single.

I stayed at Michael's for the last year or so when I could. It worked out fine. We made it work. And then, Michael proposed. It was about to become permanent.

I blinked, bringing myself back. Back to the present, I realized we were pulling up to Michael's family house. It was finally time….

Your Mom's In My Business…

Michael's parents lived in an estate that looked like something out of an old TV show like "Lifestyles of the Rich and Famous." I knew they had money, but damn, not like this. It made Michael's place look cozy.

The house sat at the end of a long driveway, perfectly manicured hedges, with a grand entrance with marble steps leading up to an oversized mahogany door.

It wasn't just wealth—it was money, money. I almost pissed myself. The kind that didn't have to prove itself. The kind that could afford to look effortless. Michael's mother inherited hers from her family, and his father made his money in banking and investments. This wasn't the Cosby's. This was like the show "Empire."

I smoothed my sleek black dress that hugged my body just enough to remind Michael's mother that I wasn't some Plain Jane that she could dismiss. But not over the top. Classy. Ebony said it's giving posh.

Ebony had helped me pick it out, insisting I go for expensive and intimidating. She knew.

"If she doesn't like you," Ebony had said, sipping her wine, "at least make sure she respects you. Some women are cruel. She just might be a bitch."

Michael led me up the stairs, his grip on my hand firm as if to brace himself for impact in a crash landing. I felt terrible for him. That should've been my first red flag. The door opened before we could knock.

And there she was. Olivia Johnson.

In her day, you could tell that she was "that girl." She was popular but sophisticated. The woman looked like she'd been carved out of ice—regal, elegant, and cold.

She was tall and thin, her gray silk dress draped over her like it had been designed specifically for her body, in contrast to her light-skinned complexion.

She had Michael's eyes, the same deep brown, but hers held none of his warmth.

She didn't smile.

"Ni---," she said started to say, her voice smooth, yet disapproving, but I stopped her.

"It's NeeNee," I corrected her, smiling sweetly.

Her eyes flickered over me, from my hair to my heels, before landing on my engagement ring.

"Shall we?" she said, stepping aside.

Michael squeezed my hand, a silent "go with it," before leading me inside. His hand briefly touched my arm.

The house smelled expensive—like leather and aged wood, with a hint of something floral lingering in the air.

Fresh flowers? I saw the garden outside.

A woman appeared from nowhere, offering a flute of champagne, but I shook my head.

I needed to be completely sober for this.

Dinner was set in a grand dining room with a table long enough to seat a small army. Good. I had come to fight if needed. I saw that disapproving look in her eyes.

Michael's father was already seated at the head of the table. Malcolm Johnson, I presumed.

As he stood up, Michael looked like he could be this man's brother, not his son.

The only thing that betrayed Malcolm's age was the gray hair in his beard. Unlike his wife, he smiled when he saw me, after he hugged his son.

"You must be the famous NeeNee," he said, shaking my hand. He got ten cool points for saying my name.

"Michael's told us so much about you."

Doubt it. Did he even talk about me?

"Nice to meet you, Mr. Johnson," I said.

"Call me Malcolm," he said, waving off the formality. I liked him instantly. He and I could be friends.

I wasn't here to win over Malcolm, though.

The real test sat across from me, watching, waiting. She reminded me of Keisha. That Keisha.

Dinner started civilly. The food was served by a maid.

Small talk, polite smiles, nothing too deep.

Then Olivia turned to me, her expression unreadable. She pursed her lips. The small talk was over.

"So, NeeNee," she said, almost as if she spit the words out, setting down her wine glass. "Tell us more about you? What do your parents do? Where are you from?"

There it was. There she was, the real her, not the fake bitch she sent in at first with all of the pleasantries.

Michael stiffened beside me like he knew this was coming. He tensed up. He was scared of her. I had never seen this side of him. It was different.

"My mother left when I was young," I said, keeping my voice even. "I never really knew her."

"And my father—" I hesitated. "Let's just say he remarried. He lives in Philadelphia."

Olivia arched a delicate brow. "I see. Is your family well known? Should I know them?"

Then, silence, like she was circling her prey.

My throat was suddenly dry. I picked up my glass and took a slow sip of water.

She was waiting for me to elaborate. She'd be waiting all night. She'd hold her breath and die before I told her about any of my weaknesses. The very things she could use later on to try to hurt me. I wasn't having that.

She smiled, but it wasn't friendly. "And what is it you do, exactly? Do you have a job? Or once you are married, will you depend on Michael. I am also curious if you know about Michael's---"

Michael looked like he saw a ghost. What was that?

"I am a publicist." I said cutting her off.

"So you are good at keeping secrets. For a firm?" She pressed on, like she was waiting for me to say I worked retail, or something. Or that I was a social media influencer selling my body. Only what? Just for who?

"Yes," I said smiling, just as sweetly. "For one of the top agencies in New York, I work with Fortune 500 companies. I started out as an intern. They love me."

Malcolm let out a low whistle. "Impressive."

Olivia's lips pressed together in a thin line.

Michael cleared his throat to speak, trying to steer the conversation somewhere less hostile. Olivia wasn't having that. She already started her shit.

"Mom, Dad, NeeNee's incredible at what she does. She's one of the most talented—"

"That's nice, dear," Olivia interrupted, her eyes still on me, and they were cocked like pistols.

I set down my fork. "Is there something you want to ask me, Mrs. Johnson? Say it!"

Michael shot me a "please don't start" look, but I was done playing nice. He could be afraid of her, but I wasn't about to sacrifice my pride.

She was one of those monsters, hiding under my bed and in my closet. I was tired of being afraid of things and people like her. Aunt Shirley. Keisha. Really tired.

Olivia tilted her head, considering a question, and then she spoke. "I suppose I'm just... curious about your intentions with our son, given his proclivities? Lord knows this family can't any more embarrassment. Malcolm, you can't always clean up his mess. He---"

Malcolm looked at his wife, "That's enough! Stop it!"

I almost choked. What the fuck was she trying to say? What about Michael? The gloves were off. She wanted a fight. I am from Philly. She doesn't know me.

"My intentions?" I laughed aloud. A low, incredulous laugh. Had Michael dated women way worse than me before? And they did something to him? To this family?

"You think I'm after his money? Your money?"

She didn't answer. She didn't have to. I leaned forward, my voice calm, but sharp, and spoke.

"Let me be clear. I don't need Michael's money. I don't need anything from this family. I make my own money, and I do just fine." I picked up my wine glass and took a sip. "So if you're waiting for me to pull out a shovel and start digging, you'll always be waiting. I love your son and that should be the only thing concerning you."

Malcolm chuckled. "I like her. Feisty."

Olivia's eyes were like ice. She expected me to be ghetto and some hood rat trash that she could dismiss. Nope. Not on duty. She started to speak and stopped.

Dinner wrapped up soon after that. Olivia was quiet after what I said to her—too quiet, but good. She kept looking at me, and at Michael. Michael was nervous.

The food was terrible anyway. The chicken was overcooked. There was no seasoning. I used to work in food services. It tasted like tree bark.

And Michael was quiet during the drive back. He didn't need to say another word. I didn't press the issue.

When we got back to my apartment, he put the car in park, but didn't turn it off. I knew he didn't want me to spend the night with him. He brought me home. He was upset—not angry—but upset—probably because I had to check his mother. This was his way of telling me.

"NeeNee," he started, rubbing his face.

I sighed. "Michael, just say it."

He seemed tired and defeated. "My mother is difficult, but you didn't have to go there."

I laughed. "Difficult? That woman practically called me a gold digger to my face. And those digs about you?"

"She'll come around," he said, his voice pleading. She just needs time. She is my mother, though. You have to show more respect. She is just being protective."

I stared at him, and I really looked at him. His shoulders were tense. I saw how he looked like he was caught between me and her. "Did you bother to protect me?"

"She's never going to accept me, is she?" I asked. "I am not from your world. Your world. This life."

Michael exhaled. "Sweetheart—"

I nodded, cutting him off. "Got it."

I reached for the door handle.

"NeeNee, don't do this."

I turned back and gave him a small, sad smile. "I didn't. You did. Your mother did. Good luck with that."

And then, I got out of the car and went inside.

And for the first time, I knew this engagement wasn't going to last. I felt like a caged bird with Michael. With Shawn, I was just me. With Michael, I had to pretend.

I looked at my engagement ring. I wanted this. I realized you have to be careful what you wish for...

No Happy Holidays…

Michael pulled away from the curb, like he pulled away from me, when things got complicated. He ghosted me. No phone calls. No texts. Just silence.

It was his way of controlling me. I thought.

I didn't hear from him that first night. Then, the inevitable silence that always came with his disappearances came the next. I could only imagine what his mother had to say about me that night.

I was used to the patterns of his disappearances. But this time, I earned it. At first, it was subtle.

A missed call here, a delayed text there.

He made plans and then "forgot" to tell me about them.

Meetings that ran long. Late nights at the office.

Then came the excuses and the avoidance.

The silence was unbearable. I'd been here before.

This time, we jumped straight to silence.

And I was tired of this Scorpio man shit.

This wasn't new. This was different though.

Michael had a pattern—one that played on a loop.

It was his way of controlling me, I guess.

He pulled me close when it was convenient, then disappeared the moment things got real.

And the worst part? I always let him come back.

I always gave him grace. I forgave him. They say in an abusive relationship; it takes seven attempts for a woman to finally leave. This was emotional abuse.

I always made room for his absences. I accepted his excuses, his "stress." What about my needs?

But this time? Something again was different.

I was angry at myself for cutting his mother off when she asked me, "Do I know about Michael's what?" What was she trying to tell me? I should have listened.

The only problem, I am over him right now.

I didn't feel like fighting for him anymore.

Here, I thought Monica was the challenge. I was fighting his mother, his precious image of himself, and his need to decide how things would play out.

I was even tired of praying. Somebody once said religion is for people afraid of hell, so I am spiritual. When you are spiritual, you have been through some shit. This was that. And the crazy part, it wasn't over by a long shot. I still haven't talked to him yet.

When I called him, his calls went straight to voicemail. Did he block my number? Or turned his phone off…

Where You At...

Ebony, her bonnet hanging halfway on her head, didn't even look up from her phone when she asked me the question.

"You don't even like him anymore?"

"Ebony, I do." It sounded like I was lying though.

I sat on the other couch, staring at my phone. I had not heard from Michael in weeks.

Ebony sipped from her glass of wine like she was watching a car crash that she'd predicted.

I hated when she did that.

"NeeNee," she said, shaking her head. "Do you hear yourself? You are lying so much you could trip over the truth and act like you didn't see it. I know you, girl."

I sighed. "Ebony—"

"No. No 'Ebony.'" She waved her hands at me, eyes narrowing. "I am so sick of this man treating you like an afterthought. Either he shits, or gets off the pot with this. Who is he, a superhero? Out fighting crime?"

I groaned, rubbing my temples. "It's—"

"Say 'complicated,'" she warned me, as she stood up, "and I will throw this wine on you."

I rolled my eyes. "I was gonna say 'temporary.'"

Ebony cackled. "Oh, girl, you a fool."

She placed her glass down dramatically.

"Michael's whole personality is temporary. His attention span? Temporary. His commitment? Temporary. Hell, I bet the credit limit on his card is temporary."

I fought a laugh.

She narrowed her eyes. "How long has it been since you even saw his ass?"

I hesitated. "Two weeks."

Her jaw dropped. "TWO WEEKS?"

I winced. "He's been busy."

"With what? Doing what? Doing who? Ghosting you? Girl, you are better than me. You should kill him."

I stayed quiet as she just called me stupid.

And that was the answer Ebony needed.

She sat down and leaned forward.

Ebony's voice was subdued now. Her eyes almost sad for me. "So I was right. You are tired of his ass."

I opened my mouth. Then I closed it.

"So what are you going to do? Are you are going to let Michael get away with his 'It is complicated excuse?'"

"I don't know. It may not be so easy."

Ebony scoffed. "Complicated, my ass. Look, men aren't complicated. They are creatures of habit. If they want you to meet their family, you meet their family. If they don't, they don't see you as family. You met his family, now what? He ghosted you just like that."

I groaned, "Well damn, tell me how you really feel. I don't want that kind of drama." I sighed.

Ebony laughed. "I did warn you. I have been telling you. and you never want any drama. Me, I want all of the smoke. You are involved with a mama's boy. And the one thing you can't beat is a boy's love for his mother. You will go from riding shotgun to sitting in the back seat every time she gets in the car."

"Now it's time to move on." Ebony looked at me and winked. "And you know what my grandmother says about how to get over one man…"

Dammit, she was right. I glanced at her. I laughed, and I lied, "I don't know."

Her smile stretched wide. "You will."

I groaned, sipping on my wine.

Ebony refilled her glass, tilting her head. "You know what we need to do tonight?"

I already knew where this was going.

I sighed. "Ebony—"

"Forget this. We are going out. Girl, I don't care what happened today. We don't even need to drink. You need a distraction. No, you need a drink drink."

I fought a smile. "We are already drinking…"

Ebony ignored me, "Girl, I keep telling you, these men ain't nothing but stress dipped in a good cologne. We might as well have some fun."

I laughed, "Not now, Ebony."

Ebony was not about to let it go. She sat down beside me, tossing her braids over her shoulders. She studied my face for a second, and then, spoke.

"So, what else are we going to do about Michael then? You are too scared to kill his stupid ass. Girl, we can either drink, we can sit here crying over him, or we are fighting him and his mama. I got my bat in my closet."

I laughed, despite myself, "None of the above. Girl, you know we don't have enough bail money. I will be fighting off all of the big chicks up in the prison with you. So stop. And wait! Is that how you handle your men?"

"Girl, I don't chase men; I trip them and then ask why they fell for me?" Ebony laughed.

"You need to be stopped." I laughed.

"I know," Ebony said dismissively. "Now decide if we do drink, are we sad drinking, or hoe drinking, to get through this, so I can decide where to go. Drinks. Music. Men who text back. This too shall pass."

I tried to protest, but Ebony was not listening, so I knew better. The decision was made.

So I got up to get dressed, wondering who wrote this tragic script that I call my life.

It can't be real.

I thought about texting Michael, but his silence should have been my red flag, and all this other stuff was the entire parade…

So You Like What You See...

An hour later, I was in a simple dress and heels, sitting in a bar full of people who looked as if they didn't have a care in the world.

Bodies moved in sync with the rhythm of the music, and the air was thick with heat, liquor, and good music.

Ebony had already ordered two shots and nudged me to take one. "You need to loosen up. Here, drink this. You need a distraction."

"I am good." I downed the shot, but I could barely taste the liquor. My mind wasn't on getting drunk.

Ebony gave me a side-eye. "Sis, you look like you are standing here waiting for a rideshare, or you are an abandoned puppy. This is Michael's loss. He is clearly afraid of his mother's opinion. That's his problem."

I exhaled. "I hate that you are right."

"I'm not right; I am real about life and what I see." Ebony was already looking around the room. "You ever look at somebody and know you are about to waste your time." Ebony's phone buzzed, but she ignored it.

I laughed despite myself.

Ebony mused, "Every one of these men reminds me why I don't have exes, just people that mistakenly audition for the lead role in my life. It's like you're praying for a sign, and God is sending you red flags, like 'girl, don't do it.'" Ebony's phone went off again.

Just then, out of the corner of my eye, I saw him. The man at the end of the bar, with skin the color of a good cup of coffee, was tall and wearing a white shirt that clung to his arms. He was just watching me.

He caught me staring, but instead of looking away, he took a sip of his drink and nodded. I smiled back.

I should have looked away. I didn't. Isn't this how it always starts? He looked like the kind of guy who sat at a bar, waiting for you to come to him. I'm not that kind of woman. I am the one who gets approached.

His eyes were dark, hooded, and dangerous. They swept over me like he was undressing me with his eyes. I looked up at him again. He smiled back.

And then, he looked away like this was nothing. Ebony saw it. I thought to myself, I am losing my touch.

"You see that man over there?" Ebony whispered, pointing to some other guy standing in a corner. "He looks like a free trial, good for a week, and then, it's time to cancel. He has been staring at me for the last ten minutes. Should I go talk to him?"

I laughed, "Do you even have to ask?"

"I am just saying you have to keep your desires high and your expectations low. It is called balance these days, sis. I know he looks toxic, but I like my love life with a little seasoning." Ebony flipped her hair and strutted off, leaving me alone at the bar.

When I looked up again, Ebony had already had that man looking, as if he was already so deep under her spell that I half-expected him to sign over his pension. Ebony didn't even do relationships. She dated, but nothing serious. Ebony was just so picky.

I saw it all through school.

She'll find somebody.

One day. Someday.

Maybe.

So when Ebony finally came back and gave me that look like she had enough for the night already, I knew. She then looked at her phone and said something about how her feet hurt; I told her to go home. She gave me that look like no, we don't leave each other, but I waived her off. I wanted to stay.

We had not been there even an hour.

Besides, the mystery man from earlier fit my type. Ebony stood there and watched us exchange glances. Between Michael and Shawn, you'd think it was somebody with a great smile and emotionally unavailable. Ebony left and he was still there waiting.

I looked at my phone and I think I lost track of time as I waited for him to do or say something. Anything. It didn't happen. So, I listened to a few songs that played. A few made me think about Shawn. And then, I remembered my mystery man. I looked up to check in on him. Damn, he was gone just that fast.

Yeah, I lost my touch...

Superpowers...

By the time Ebony texted me a half hour later, I realized how much I needed this change of scene. To be outside. I just refused to tell her that. It gave me time to think and to decide what to do about Michael. I didn't know what to do. I was tired of him. She was right.

I had just ordered a soda when I felt a presence. It was a man. I smelled his cologne before I saw him.

I felt a heat in my back. No, I wasn't drunk.

I didn't bother to turn around, figuring he was the mystery man looking bored at the end of the bar earlier. Now, he was finally standing here.

Somehow, he managed to get up and find the courage to come and talk to me. He was trying to be smooth, but coming off corny. So I played along. But, for the first time that night, I felt... different. Nervous. I didn't know why. It was crazy. Everything in me said to run.

He leaned in slightly, and the scent of something intoxicating eloped around me. I smiled. Maybe I hadn't lost my touch. He was here after all of those looks across the bar. Ebony had even seen it.

"Looks like your guy at the end of the bar left you." His voice was warm and deep. "His loss. Can I buy you a drink to make it up to you?"

I hesitated. That voice?

"What makes you think I need anyone to buy me a drink? I am a big girl. I am grown." I teased.

I heard him laugh. "I can see that. But, you looked like a woman about to make a bad decision. I want to help you make a better one. Maybe even with me."

I laughed out loud. "Wow! That's your line? Your super powers don't seem to be working on me?"

"I didn't have time to prepare. I could have said something smoother, like seeing you improved my day. I had to argued with a pigeon this morning. Or something silly like do you think Jesus learned to walk on water as a baby when he didn't want a bath?"

Corny, but I laughed. And I turned around.

It was the last person I expected to see…

Shawn. Shawn Jonathan Conquest.

That Shawn. Shawn Shawn.

Just like in college, he always turned up where I was. It drove me crazy in school as if he had a tracking device on my hip.

There are millions of people in this city alone, and yet, here he was. I should've gone home.

I should have told him that I have a man. I should have run. Instead, I did the one thing I never did.

I stayed, when I should have left him right there…

Do You Remember…

I watched Shawn watching me. It was really him.

I had to look again because he seemed older.

More mature. Not that young man that I knew.

His hair was still curly, with the sides tapered.

That same mischievous smile

And those eyes.

He was no longer that guy who drove me crazy in class.

He was a grown-ass man.

My stomach dropped. It did backflips.

That skin, his crisp lineup, and his tailored suit made it clear he was doing well for himself and how he bit his lip. I missed all of that. I missed him.

At first, I thought I was dreaming, but this was real.

Our eyes locked, and I stopped breathing.

His lips parted slightly, and I couldn't move.

His whole expression shifted from silliness to something else—something intense.

I panicked. I looked away, but only for a minute.

I trembled like I had just seen a ghost.

Too late. I was shaken. He had me.

Then, he touched me subtly at my waist.

And I didn't stop him.

"Hey, NeeNee!" His voice was smooth as ever.

It felt like time stood still since the last time I saw him on his graduation day. It felt like a lifetime ago.

The way he said it, my name still did something dangerous to me.

I swallowed hard, gripping my phone. "Shawn."

He smirked. "Been a minute."

I nodded. "Yeah."

His eyes dragged over me, slow and deliberate. "You look good."

I forced a small smile. "So do you."

Shawn tilted his head, studying me.

"Are you alone? Or are you waiting for the guy?"

How long had he been watching me to know that?

"You just literally missed Ebony," I replied.

Shawn chuckled. "Some things never change. Damn, and I miss her too. Is she still short?"

I let out a small laugh. "Nope. She is six foot five."

Shawn laughed, then silence stretched between us. Not awkward. Just… charged. His eyes softened.

My throat tightened. "I still owe you a real apology after all of these years. I apologize…"

Shawn raised a brow. "We are grown grown now. It's in the past. I forgive you if you will forgive me. If anything, I apologize again to you."

I looked down at my phone. "It's not that."

Shawn took a sip of his drink and let me finish.

"I shouldn't have shut you out. I was selfish. It was yours too. I never thought about what you were actually feeling at the time. I apologize." I said finally.

"I got help. Dealt with it. Apology accepted." He replied.

"You didn't deserve that," I continued, but relieved.

"We didn't." He corrected me. "I understand."

This isn't something that needed to be said in a crowded bar. But I thought this might be my last time seeing him. So I tried it. I had to.

Shawn changed the subject for both of us. I was glad he did. "And now? How are you? Are you single, married, or divorced?"

"It's complicated." I held up my hand and showed him my engagement ring.

He let out a low, knowing chuckle.

"Same. Complicated." He held up a hand with a wedding band. He nodded, looking away briefly before locking eyes with me again. "I wear this for show. It's actually a nice ring and it keeps some ladies off me."

I smiled politely, "You don't have to explain."

Shawn looked at me again, "NeeNee, I should."

Suddenly, it felt like we weren't in this bar. We were back in college. Back in my dorm room, tangled in my sheets, whispering lies and promises that neither of us was brave enough to keep. I remembered all of it.

Shawn took a step closer. Not touching me again. Not yet. But close enough to make my heart pound.

I felt the heat between us.

His voice dropped, as he moved closer. "So you really stopped running, NeeNee, long enough for somebody to finally catch you? I love that for you."

My breath hitched. My mind said move, bitch.

"I'm trying to." I knew I was lying when I said the words. Then I asked, "Are you happy?"

Shawn looked at me and said the words that would haunt me, "No. Not since you..."

208

Snooze…

What did he just say? Run, NeeNee! His jaw tightened, and something flashed in his eyes. He took another sip of his drink. I didn't want to ask. I just let him talk

"I thought when you stopped running, it would be with me. I would be enough to make you stop, and you'd be with me." Shawn said almost sheepishly.

Damn it, Shawn! And he looked good.

Could he tell that Michael and I were having problems?

He leaned in, his voice rough, full of something unspoken. "Are you happy?"

I wanted to tell him the truth. No.

But it was too late to stop this.

That I had moved on from him regardless.

But the words wouldn't come.

Because the truth? I wasn't sure if I had.

And Shawn knew it. He had to sense and feel it.

A woman walked toward us, and I thought, "This is it. It's his wife."

Thank you, Mrs. Conquest. Come get your husband!

But Shawn merely introduced her as his business associate's wife. The husband came over and told Shawn that they were leaving, thanking him.

It was the last of a group that he had met for drinks. They were finishing their drinks when Shawn came to talk to me, I later learned.

Shawn made the brief introduction.

I don't remember their names.

I didn't care. It wasn't his wife.

I didn't even care about her name.

Shawn licked his lips and asked the one question I wasn't expecting.

"So where were we…"

The Truth…

I should have walked away. Instead I, stayed with Shawn. I should have told him again that I have a man. Instead, I got lost in how his eyes lingered on my lips.

The way his fingers brushed against my hips when we danced. The way his fingers brushing against my skin sent shivers down my spine.

And I knew, in that moment, that whatever happened next, I wouldn't be able to take it back. This wasn't a dream. This was real.

His gaze didn't waver. It didn't flinch.

It didn't apologize for the way it stripped me bare in the middle of a crowded bar.

One drink turned into two more.

Those two drinks turned words.

Smooth conversation, easy laughter that turned into his lips on mine. Yes, we kissed.

Maybe it was the alcohol.

Perhaps it was the frustration from Michael's distance. It could have been something more profound. Something deeper that I didn't want to name. Love?

I could be myself with Shawn like I could never be that way with Michael. I felt safe. With Michael, I was guarded. With Shawn, I felt protected.

I missed this.

I missed Shawn.

When he looked at me, I let him watch me. And that voice with a slight Southern accent.

His voice was smooth, velvety, with just the right amount of danger. I swallowed harsh. Nervous. He smirked. My pulse was hammering in my ears.

"Are you always still this smooth?" I asked.

His smile deepened. "Only when it counts and gets me what I want. I want to be with you tonight."

When we finally sat down, I let him sit next to me. His body was close, familiar, and warm.

His voice became low, warm, teasing, and inviting.

I let him make me forget—for a little while—that I was mad as hell at Michael, and questioning everything about my relationship. This is what I let walk away?

I was feeling more lost than I wanted to admit.

Michael never came up in the conversation.

Neither did his Shawn's wife. Not even her name.

If it did, I don't remember it at all.

I don't remember when we left the bar.

I don't remember the cab ride.

I don't remember how I followed him into his dimly lit hotel room. I texted Ebony to let her know I was okay and gave her my location. She didn't reply.

I remembered his hands, though.

The way they roamed over my skin, slow, deliberate, like he made love to me from memory.

I remember his mouth. He spelled out his name, his whole name, on my body with his tongue.

The way it found me in the dark, hungry, desperate, tasting of whiskey, and something sweeter, something forbidden. Infidelity maybe.

I belonged to him for one night, and he belonged to me, if only for this one night.

We barely made it to the bed for round two, clothes forgotten, skin burning. It happened.

I let him take me, pull me under, drowning me in the kind of pleasure that I hadn't felt in a long time. His love was like comfort food. Warm and satisfying.

Filling and familiar. But I was still hungry.

It was everything, heat, hunger, and home. It was like making up for lost time. It wasn't Michael.

I didn't think about Michael. Why should I?

I didn't think about tomorrow. I needed now.

I didn't think about anything but the way Shawn felt, the way he moved, and the way he made me forget everything but this. Just like he always did.

And when it was over, the room was quiet, except for the sound of our ragged breaths, just like in college.

The bed was just bigger.

I lay in the dark, staring at the ceiling, with reality creeping back in. Why now? Why him?

I had just cheated on Michael.

The very thing I had once accused Michael of doing to me. Ain't that some shit? It is what it is.

I didn't care.

And the worst part?

I wasn't even sure I regretted it....

I'm So Into You...

The next morning, sunlight streamed into the room, warm and intrusive.

The sheets were soft.

The kind that costs money.

I woke up slowly. I could smell him on my skin.

Then I felt it.

The warmth of another body.

That's when I heard him.

Slowly. Cautiously. I turned my head, and there he was. Shawn. Shawn Shawn.

You said it in your head. I know you did.

Shawn Jonathan Conquest.

Shawn Shawn.

Ebony was right. I didn't always say his name twice because saying it matched the beat of my heart.

Shawn had my heart.

Shawn lay beside me still. His face relaxed in sleep. His bare chest rose and fell with steady breaths.

Suddenly, panic clawed at my throat.

Oh, shit. This is Shawn. Shawn Shawn!

I needed to go! Now! Run! I can't do this!

As I pulled the sheets to me, I pulled them off him, exposing him, and waking him at the same time.

Shawn looked at me with a smile.

"Good morning, Baby. Tell me you weren't about to leave before breakfast. You know I got to eat."

My stomach twisted. I couldn't do this.

I couldn't just sit there and pretend this wasn't what it was. "Girl, he is married," I could hear Ebony say.

My night should have ended with a hug.

Nothing more. Not glazed like a honey bun.

Instead, it was a moment of weakness. A moment of sin that I couldn't take back.

And there he was, staring at me—Shawn, propped up on one elbow, watching. His voice was warm and deep, and his expression was one of happiness.

I didn't panic anymore. I laid back down.

At first, I just lay there blinking at the ceiling, trying to piece together the night before.

My head was pounding, my body a mess of dull aches in the best way, but beneath all of that was something worse. I had the unsettling feeling this was exactly where I needed to be and always wanted to be.

Shawn shifted.

His deep brown eyes were now locked on me.

That lazy smile was still playing on his lips

"You good?" His voice was still smooth, like he had all the time in the world, but I wasn't "good."

I gave a nod and slowly sat up, pulling the covers around me and off him more.

I looked around, trying to distract myself from him.

The room was expensive. Not just nice, expensive. Sleek. Modern furniture. Michael would love this place.

Damn it, Michael!

It had floor-to-ceiling windows that overlooked the city. Shawn's family had money, but he differed from Michael's "rich." The crisp white sheets smelled like fresh laundry and expensive cologne.

The kind of place a man like Shawn now belonged.

Me? I didn't belong here at all. Just like with Michael, I didn't need a lot. Now I realize why I compared Michael to Shawn. It was because they were alike in a lot of ways. But with Michael, he thrived on status and this and that, whereas Shawn lived like a broke college kid, and very little used to impress him. Well, it didn't.

I turned to Shawn. "I, I don't usually do this."

He laughed, "Anymore, or like we used to?"

He stretched, his muscles flexing in a way that made my stomach do a backflip.

I should have left right then, but I didn't move.

I should have gathered my clothes, done the walk of shame, and tried to forget any of this ever happened. Instead, I sat there staring at him. He saw me.

After all of the bullshit we had been through, how I treated him, he was here like nothing happened. How?

Either way, he would only be in town for a few days and would be gone soon enough. We didn't talk about that.

I used to think Shawn's father was just some executive and that Shawn was given a job. I learned his father owned the company last night, which explained the hotel room and why Shawn bullshitted in school.

He could afford to. When he paid for last night with a platinum American Express card in his own name and the year was the same year that he turned 19, I asked. Wouldn't you? He just laughed it off. Now this.

Shawn did say he was in New York working on several projects that he spearheaded. How he was happy he had paid attention to business law. I smiled.

He grinned. "I need that last night. I need you."

That answer! That should have been my cue to run. There was something in his eyes that made me pause. We still had a connection. It was still there.

It was like he knew something that I didn't.

"Shawn, I..." I tried to say what I was feeling.

Instead, I let myself watch him for one second too long. And that second? He used it well and against me.

He put a finger to my lips and said, "Stop. Whatever you are about to say. Stop. Right now, give me this moment so that when you go back to him, I want to ruin every thought that you have that doesn't include me. Now, lay back down. Let me finish what I started."

That was all it took to change everything. He used that next second to reach over and touch me again, and in that brief instance, I allowed it to destroy every bit of resistance that I had left. I needed this too.

And we did it again...

And then, again...

He did that thing where he spelled out his whole name with his tongue again. Shawn Jonathan Conquest...

Never Keeping Secrets...

I spent the entire cab ride back home trying to talk myself down from the ledge of shame.

It was almost two in the afternoon.

I snuck out when he was asleep. It was just one night, I said. It didn't mean anything. I lied.

Maybe I will never have to see him again.

Not one of those thoughts stopped my hands from shaking as I dug through my purse for my keys. Shawn, despite the shower where he joined me, Shawn's scent was still all over me. Did I still love him?

None of those thoughts had stopped my stomach from twisting when I thought about Michael, about the way things had gone silent. How distant he had been.

By the time I stumbled back to the apartment, Ebony was already waiting for me, arms crossed, face twisted in pure amusement like that night in my dorm room. She gave me that look, just like back in school.

Ebony looked at me and raised an eyebrow, looking like somebody's mother.

Ebony was being Ebony. "Well, well, well. Look who finally decided to come home. You look like a walking regret with a pulse. Like a plot twist and a red flag."

I sighed, tossing my purse on the couch. "Ebony, please! I don't want to talk about it."

"Oh, hell, no! What did you do?"

I rolled my eyes and kicked off my heels, "Good afternoon to you, too."

"Don't 'good afternoon' me," she said. "You look like you just did something you have no business doing. With your..." She hesitated, and then I sighed.

Ebony gasped. "NeeNee"

I groaned, covering my face. "Don't"

"Tell me you didn't go home with that guy from the bar. Did you have sex, or were you assembling furniture from Ikea? It's should've not taken this long for you---"

Silence. It was a guy. Not him.

Ebony screamed. "Bitch."

"Ebony, please!"

"No, no, you don't get to 'Ebony please' me after dropping something like that on me. What the hell? Girl, he could have been crazy. Deranged. We had these talks about strangers. At least tell me it was that good."

I ran my hands through my hair. "It just... happened. I don't know. We talked and--"

"Sex doesn't just happen, NeeNee. You choose it. You actively participated. Stop that." She threw her hands up. "Damn, I should have never left you at that bar with your hot ass. All of y'all out here being fresh."

221

"It was a mistake. It didn't mean anything."

Ebony folded her arms. "That's what you told him? Girl, you have no couth. Was it good?"

I hesitated. "...Yeah."

Ebony let out a long, exaggerated whistle. "Damn, it was good, and you still just left my boy with nothing but a memory, huh? You are scandalous."

I gave her a look, "Your boy?"

"I mean, I don't know him, but I should be on his side with this. He wakes up thinking he made an impression, and you hit him with that." She shook her head. "Cold-blooded. But, I am not mad at you."

I groaned, "Can we not do this right now?"

"Okay! I have just one question." She leaned forward. "But for real, did he put it down like that? Because you got that 'I was up all night' glow" like you used to have with the one whose name we don't say. Ain't seen that look on your face in years! I am impressed."

Just then, I realized she was talking about Shawn. Ooh, I couldn't tell her it was him. At least not yet. She would say she told me so, even after all these years.

I'm not saying shit.

What? So I can't tell her the truth about that part without telling her who it was. I could still feel his hands on me, hear the way his voice wrapped around me in the dark, and remember how he made me forget all of my problems. And it was Shawn Shawn. Our Shawn.

So I swallowed hard and muttered, "Yes."

"Bitch, I knew you had it in you," Ebony began to whoop so loud that I thought the neighbors might complain. "Good for you, girl. I am just glad for your one hall pass from Michael, and that it wasn't boyfriend dick."

I sat up, "What is boyfriend dick?"

"Let me find out I didn't teach anything. Class is in session," Ebony laughed. "It's when the dick is good for a relationship, but if it were a one-night stand, you'd be less than impressed. It's regular. Now vacation dick is when you can only take it like you would a vacation. You know, not all of the damn time, or sober."

I laughed, and Ebony tugged at her bonnet because she was serious. "Boyfriend dick can't date big girls because the stomach-to-dick ratio is not there once you get past the fupa. The fat upper pussy area."

I hollered. "Shut up."

Ebony laughed. "Boyfriend dick say, 'Let me know if I am hurting you,' and you think it's a finger."

"No, this was different," I laughed, and then, I was suddenly serious. "Ebony, I needed that."

Ebony did a fake gasp, "Oh, you are a hoe now? Who are you, and where is my friend? Girl, stop!"

"Shut up." I laughed. Still, I wasn't ready to tell Ebony that it was Shawn. Our Shawn. I didn't have the strength, time, or the energy.

"So, what's next? Are you hitting him up again? To find out if he has a brother for me?"

"I don't know. I just… I need to figure things out." And by "things," I meant Michael.

As much as I hated to admit it, part of me still wasn't ready to let him go…

Revenge…

I didn't call Shawn. I wasn't ready. Instead, I decided to go to Michael's the next day after work. You know, surprise him. I tried to call, but I got his voicemail.

As much as I was curious about this new Shawn, this more mature version, I had to put away childish feelings. He was married. I am engaged.

Maybe Shawn would realize it was a one-time thing if I didn't call him back. I did text him a thank you.

He lives in Atlanta. I'm here.

Not to mention, Shawn had a whole wife. Shawn.

She probably was sweet and deserved an apology.

We never really talked about her, but she existed.

This may have been the wake-up call I needed. I was ready to move on to a future with Michael. If need be, I would learn to tolerate his mother. His father was a lovely man. Maybe he would protect me from her.

As I walked into Michael's apartment building, I got that same sinking feeling walking into his mother's house.

My fingers trembled as I slid my key into Michael's apartment door. I didn't know why. I felt like even his doorman gave me an odd look. He knew something.

Maybe he knew that I had not used these keys in weeks, that things had been off since his mother's house. Now, I was ready to talk, and, to be honest, to commit to Michael. Also, I felt guilty for cheating on him.

The lock on his apartment door clicked open. I stepped inside, closing the soft-close door behind me.

The lights were dim, and the air was thick with the faint smell of Michael's cologne mixed with something else.

They clashed, but I was smelling something else. Sex.

I walked through the open space, and my heels were quiet as soft music played nearby.

A half-empty bottle of rum sat on the counter. There were empty glasses next to it.

Then, I saw the clothes, too many to be just Michael's, tossed all over the living room. Was Michael having a slumber party? Let's get everyone out of bed.

Then, there were empty condom wrappers.

Good to know. Let me still get another checkup.

I took a deep breath to calm my nerves.

A slow breath left my lips.

I wasn't the type to make assumptions, but my gut already knew. Still, I had to see for myself.

My blood ran cold as I moved towards the bedroom. The door was slightly ajar, enough to let the soft moans from inside, slip out. Michael's moan was one of them.

Pushing the door open just enough, I saw them.

Not him. Them. They didn't even notice me.

I held my breath, not to give myself away.

I was so wrong. He used me to keep his mother from finding out about.... this shit. Or maybe she knew and was trying to warn me about it. Damn.

What word did she use? Proclivities?

If she didn't know, he couldn't tell her about this.

She'd kill over. You might not know the way her face looked. Like it had already been set in stone.

And now this? My gut knew not to trust him.

They were tangled in silk sheets that I used to sleep in. Michael's sweaty back glistened, and a slow, satisfying moan left his lips. He was enjoying himself, no doubt.

I just watched him perform like in a circus.

I needed to be sure. I was not hurt. I wasn't angry. I wasn't. I didn't cry? What could a tear fix?

Just a quiet realization came over me.

This is who he is. This is what he is. Big Mike.

Maybe this was a sexual addiction? His drug of choice. I had only heard stories about things like this, both men and women, but you never know what beats in some people's hearts, and in their minds. Nobody ever asks.

227

This man made me feel like I had to be good enough to earn a spot in his world. This is how he moved when he thought nobody was watching. My gut was right.

It wasn't even Monica. I didn't know them, and that is what made him so good at hiding this. I couldn't pick them out of a lineup, and yet, they seemed to be comfortable in this place. They had been here before.

When, though? And of everything, I accused him of…

It wasn't even just another woman.

There were three of them.

Michael. Her. And him. Yeah, I said it.

All in bed together. And the look on Michael's face. I couldn't see their faces. That is what surprised me.

I didn't gasp. I didn't cry. I had seen enough.

I didn't slam a door, or make a scene.

I turned around, walked back out the way I came, and let myself out. I didn't run, though.

I left the key next to the bottle on the counter and slid my ring off my finger to keep it company until he came up for air. And don't say what you would have done.

You can't speak on it until it happens to you. Should've, could've, would've doesn't count in the real world. Stop lying to yourself. No, no, no. You're lying. Lower your tone and relax your pride and ask is it worth it?

Say it until you finally believe it. I learned to do it.

People will say things like they were about to slap them, or beat that person's ass. That fight will consist of a few hits until someone breaks it up, or shoots them. And then what? So, they can say they got into a fight?

That they cursed somebody out. That they beat somebody's up. No, they let somebody hurt their feelings and their response to their stupidity was anger.

And Michael, he can throw away anything I had left at his place. It wasn't much anyway. I'm over this and him.

I heard the lock click behind me on my way out. I had no reason to go back there. I was through.

I didn't even want to know why as I walked across the lobby. I just went home. I was glad I still had it.

And then, it hit me like a ton of bricks. His mother knew. And it was her that pressured him to find somebody. She just didn't count on it being me. Did she think she could control me and him? Or him through me?

Hoping it would change him. "Fix" him. If she knew what I knew, and what I just saw, good luck with that.

I was still asking myself was that even a woman upstairs? Let his mother sort that shit out...

Woman To Woman...

Michael never did call me again. I was glad.

He knew that I knew. He found the ring and my key.

When my phone rang days later, it was Shawn. He was overly excited and still in town, and he wanted to see me before he had to leave when I answered.

Against my better judgment, I felt the same.

He said he had been busy. I wanted to see him.

Later, I checked Shawn's text for the room number. He said his meeting wrapped up early and that he was almost at the hotel. He suggested I meet him.

I caught my reflection in the lobby mirror. I had to remind myself that he was married, even if I was no longer engaged, not to touch him.

Everything in me said I shouldn't have gone to his room. We could have met up somewhere else. A bar. A lounge. A park. A restaurant.

I should have waited for him in the lobby, but my feet still carried me to the elevator and to his room.

I was being stupid. I know, but still.

I eventually stood there outside his hotel room, and that feeling of dread got me.

My hand hovered near the door, about to knock. I closed my eyes, inhaled, and told myself this was just about closure. I am not going to be a side chick.

I thought seeing him again—seeing him, period—would remind me why we couldn't be together. I thought whatever pull I felt towards him was just nostalgia, nothing more, after Michael.

I knocked. The door swung open too fast. And instead of Shawn— Keisha opened the door. I know. Keisha, right? That Keisha.

She looked surprised as if she were expecting someone else. Shawn perhaps? She stood there, all smug, smirking, and messy curls, leaning against the door frame like she had every damn right to be here.

My stomach dropped. Where were her clothes? She was dressed in a silk robe. What was that about?

She crossed her arms, tilting her head. "Oh, wow. NeeNee. Hey girl! It has been a minute?"

I hated how my name sounded in her mouth.

I fought to keep my face neutral. "Keisha."

It was her. Older, but that same bitch.

Her smirk widened. "What brings you here?"

I licked my lips, trying to think. "I was looking for Shawn. He texted me." She didn't know? But she was here.

Her expression changed. "That's funny." She gave a slight shrug. "Because you found me."

Something twisted in my stomach.

I shook my head. "Is he here?"

Keisha stepped back slightly, just enough for me to see into the room—the king-sized bed, the unzipped suitcase, the familiarity of it all. It was just her.

It was only men's clothing, though.

He wasn't here, but why was she here?

Something sharp settled in my chest.

I swallowed. Hard.

Keisha sighed dramatically. "No, but now that you are here. You know, it's funny. I didn't think you'd still be checking for Shawn after all these years. I thought you moved on. I mean it would be better for all of us, given what happened. You know. Your little accident."

Was she talking about my baby? She knew. She had to know. It was all over campus back then. And did this bitch really go there about my baby? I was heated.

She leaned against the door again, and then, with a sigh, she said, "Now that he is my husband."

My heart stopped. What did she just say?

She had to be lying. I realized I never asked.

Shawn wouldn't—But the way she was smiling…

The way she was waiting for my reaction…

I refused to give her one. I wanted to hurt her feelings. Instead, I squared my shoulders, forcing my expression into something unreadable.

"That's right?" Keisha's smile stretched wider. "Mmm-hmm. We got married years ago after his graduation."

She sighed, crossing her arms. "It's true what they say. Some women just can't let go. I have been keeping his bed warm for you all of these years."

I wanted to slap that smirk off her face, but I refused to let her see me sweat. She wasn't good enough for that. Instead, I smiled and cooed, "It must eat you up inside that you have his name, but not his heart."

Her face dropped, and she was shaken. I had to remind her that I am from Philly, and we don't play that.

I stepped closer and said, "You didn't know? And I recently fucked him too. Repeatedly. So much for keeping his bed warm. Just like I fucked him in college. Repeatedly. You knew that. You came second if you came at all. And that little accident was Shawn's baby. Now that you know, go kill yourself, you dumb bitch."

She didn't say a word. What could she say?

And then, I turned and walked away. When I glanced back, she was still standing there stuck. I know, kill yourself, bitch. I was wrong. I don't advocate self harm, but she earned that. I was done with her and Shawn…

233

Given A Chance...

I didn't cry. I didn't let myself feel anything until I was back in the lobby, gripping my handbag so hard that my knuckles turned white. That should've been the end of it. First, Michael, now Shawn married Keisha. Why?

It should've been all of the proof I needed to leave Shawn exactly where he belonged—in the past, just like I did with Michael and all of his bullshit.

Moments later, I walked out of the elevator, still trying to collect my thoughts. I thought about it, but I couldn't call Ebony. I still didn't tell Ebony that it was Shawn, who I slept with. I don't even know why I was lying to her? Out of fear? Judgment. Now this?

My mind was replaying the way Keisha's eyes had flickered—just slightly—when she spoke.

Like she wanted me to be hurt again. That was spite.

Just then, I heard my name.

"NeeNee."

I looked up. And there he was. Shawn.

He had just rushed into the lobby. His jaw clenched when he saw my face. Then he studied my face.

He knew something was wrong.

He didn't know what it was.

"Wait! Are you leaving?" he asked? "I just got here. We need to talk. Can you give me a minute?"

I swallowed. "I just saw Keisha. Your wife?"

His lips pressed together. "What is she doing here? NeeNee, wait, I can explain."

I laughed, but it sounded wrong. "That you married her anyway? After everything, you still married her. You still wanted to be with her."

Shawn exhaled sharply, raking a hand over his face. "NeeNee, it's not what it looks like…"

I held up a hand. "Save it. I shouldn't have come here. I should have trusted my gut. My mother was right."

"Wait." His voice stopped me like it always did.

I shook my head, my laugh turning hollow. "I believed you. What was I thinking? You married her! And she brought up our baby. That is a no no, Shawn."

His eyes flashed. "Wait! She did what? I got this!"

"Do you? After that bullshit you said at the bar," I scoffed. "About me running. About you being here."

I turned away, shaking my head. "Was it just for old time's sake? Damn, I'm an idiot. I feel so dumb."

Shawn cursed under his breath, stepping closer. "NeeNee, she just sold you some bullshit."

I blinked. "Excuse me?"

He clenched his jaw. "She's not my wife." His voice lowered. "She's my ex. So go ahead and believe her."

I froze. Wait! What did he say?

His eyes burned into mine. "She's only here to sign our divorce papers. We haven't been together in years. I married her out of obligation, thinking she was pregnant. My Dad tried to stop me. I didn't listen. I haven't fucked her since college. I married her, found out she lied on our wedding night, and been fighting her family ever since. So go ahead and believe her."

"With God as my witness, she wasn't even pregnant, and she has been fighting me ever since. I just literally met with my lawyer about all of this mess. I wore that ring until it was over, because he told me to. She tried to have sex with me so she really could get pregnant. Who the fuck does that? I have never lied to you."

My breath hitched.

Shawn's eyes pleaded his case. "I didn't reach out to you to start something. I just needed to see you again. I was packing to go back to Atlanta to wrap up some things. I am moving to New York to get away from her petty ass. Remember how we used to talk about this place, NeeNee. I was coming here for you."

I remembered, but still said... "And then what? You still chose her after everything we had been through? You married her, Shawn."

"Because, NeeNee, I never got to say what I wanted to you. You broke my heart in two, and shut me out after the baby, despite us. I thought she was pregnant."

My heart squeezed. "I know. I did that to you. To us. To our baby. I apologized for that. I will keep apologizing."

Shawn shook his head. "That didn't mean I stopped loving you. And that night after the bar… Damn it, NeeNee, you know how I feel about you. I still love you, and I always will. Why is this so complicated for us?"

"Because you married her," I whispered.

"Because you shut me out," he whispered." You are doing it right now. She lied. She can't let go. I did."

He took a deep breath and moved closer.

"Remember, on my graduation day, letting you walk away like that tore me apart. My love for you couldn't hold up everything we were breaking under. It would have ruined both of us, if we had let it. Not having you destroyed me. You didn't want me anymore."

"It wouldn't change anything that happened." I finally replied, refusing to cry at this moment.

"I get that, but I still love you," Shawn pleaded.

"It wasn't enough. You chose her." My heart ached.

Shawn took another step closer. "You are enough for me. You think I'd do that to you? To try to hurt you."

His voice was soft, desperate. "You think I'd move on, marry her, and then show up here just to hurt you again like I did in college. To bring up everything that almost killed me. Come on. You know me better than that."

Did I? I knew who I wanted him to be.

My heart wanted to believe him.

But my head… after Michael.

I closed my eyes. "It doesn't matter."

Shawn's entire body went still.

His voice was hoarse. "Wait! What?"

I inhaled sharply. He tried to reach out to me, and I moved. I wouldn't let him touch me. Not now.

"It doesn't matter if it's true or not. I shouldn't have come here. What was I thinking?"

His jaw flexed. "That you love me. That I love you."

"I have to go," I said.

Shawn looked at me, defeated, and finally said it.

He said, "Okay."

Something about that simple word made my chest ache.

"But do you want to?" He reached out to me. I allowed his fingertips to brush my hand. No. Absolutely not.

Shawn's eyes darkened. I knew what that warning meant, what would come next if I didn't move. I would want to stay. To be with him.

I smelled him as he moved close enough to smell the scent of him, soap, cologne, and something that had always been just him. Was it his love for me?

I stepped back, just a step. Shawn nodded again, but his eyes told a different story this time. Defeat. He had finally given up, and the most painful way to prove how much he loved me was to finally let me go.

After Michael. Monica. His mother. Shawn. Keisha. I realized I had enough. Whoever was praying for me, they needed to stop, because they were saying the wrong shit. I looked away. "Goodbye, Shawn."

He called after me, "Whenever you stop running, I will still be here waiting for you. I love you. I told you."

And I left. I couldn't do this. I know you are probably asking why the hell does she keep running? You wanted me to act a fool at Michael's, but you want me to give Shawn another chance. I am tired of being number two, or a consolation prize, after some bullshit.

You are probably also saying, "Wait until she tells Ebony! Ebony is going to flip out!" You know how Ebony feels about Shawn and about me.

Have you just ever been tired of going through shit? Can I live? Can I be what they say is great? This is not a Lifetime movie? Where is my happy ending? Mine…

"I'd Rather Be Alone...

I was through with love. I didn't want to be friends with "like," or even friendly. I went to work and came home. But, Ebony, Ebony wasn't having that after the first couple of days. After weeks of silence from me, she said I needed some air early Saturday morning.

I should've been curled up in bed with a pint of ice cream or let Ebony talk her shit from the comfort of the couch. But Ebony was persistent, so we went to brunch. I finally decided to tell Ebony everything, with no interruptions. She promised I could. She lied.

Ebony sat across from me after we ordered, watching me like a good movie. I ignored her steady gaze and tried to tell her what had happened.

"Wait. Wait." She held her hand up, blinking like I had dropped a bomb on her lap. "So you're telling me that you snuck over to Shawn's hotel after all of that—"

"Don't do that." I pointed a warning finger. "Do not make it sound like I was sneaking around looking for him. I got morals and shit."

Ebony smirked behind her mimosa. "You went to his hotel and didn't tell me, heifer. How did he look?"

I exhaled deeply, rolling my eyes. "Can you let me finish? You said no interruptions. And he's fine."

"That's my future ex-husband. Carry on." Ebony motioned for me to continue, still smirking.

"Anyway. Keisha answered the door, talking about 'Shawn's my husband' and all this extra bullshit." I said in a mocking, deep voice.

Ebony slammed her hands down. "Lies!"

I nodded. "Right? So, I was like, okay, cool. That's my cue to—"

"Wait, hold up, hold up." Ebony sat up straighter, eyes wide with excitement. "Did you slap her?"

I frowned. "What? No. You always want to fight?"

Ebony clicked her tongue. "Well, that was your first mistake. You waste too many chances to handle your business. Keisha. Monica. Throw hands next time."

I shook my head, fighting a laugh.

"You are so damn messy."

"Absolutely." Ebony sipped her drink like she wasn't currently rooting for violence. "So then what happened?"

I sighed, swirling my glass. "Shawn found me in the lobby and said Keisha was lying, that they're divorcing, and she was only here to sign the papers. That's what he called me for. She got him to marry here after graduation because she lied about being pregnant."

Ebony narrowed her eyes. "How convenient! Hmm."

"Hmm." I repeated, raising an eyebrow.

Ebony took another sip of her drink, studying me. "So lemme get this straight. He shows up in town, after all these years, looking like a goddamn romance novel cover model and my future ex-husband."

I choked on my drink. "What?"

Ebony ignored me. "He finds out you're with Michael, but still shoots his shot. You find out he has a wife, but only because he still wears his ring. But you don't ask no questions. What is the mother-fletching problem? And if he said he didn't sleep with her again, now you know why she has been acting so crazy."

Ebony continues, "He already blew your back out again for old-time sake. Then, when you reject him, he lets you walk away, but not before saying some smooth-ass, 'whenever you stop running' line? Girl, bye."

I shifted uncomfortably. "I—"

I blinked. "I mean… yeah."

Ebony tilted her head, pursing her lips. "And you believed her over him? All she had to do was show identification and say she was his wife to a copy of the room key. I have done that shit before."

I opened my mouth, and then, I closed it. I didn't know.

Ebony looked at me before downing her mimosa. "That's right, close your mouth."

Because the truth is I didn't know why I left.

"Ebony," I exhaled. "I don't know…"

Ebony looked at me, "I can't help you on this one. You are going to let him get away. It is clear you two stubborn asses belong together, just like I said, and you can't even see it."

I avoided Ebony's gaze, but she didn't let up.

"Have you ever noticed that he always managed to pop up where you were? Just like in school? I never told him. It's like you two are bonded by fate. And yet, you are running like Forrest Gump. You are crazy."

This was the new improved Ebony. Ebony 2.0.

As always, she was right.

I looked at Ebony, "I just walked out of some bullshit. I don't want to depend on anybody else to make me happy ever again. It might feel good on the lonely nights, but I need to be selfish this time. I'd rather be alone than be this unhappy. Maybe I need to be single and get my shit together before I try to do anything."

Ebony looked at me, and then she said something I should have said to myself...

You Don't Have To Worry…

Ebony groaned, throwing her head back. "Girl, I swear to God. Look at me when you lie to me, so I will know what it looks like, NeeNee. You need to stop playing, girl. You are scared of being hurt. We all are."

"Look, it's not even about that," I admitted. "It's about me. I can't keep doing this. I can't keep getting tangled up in some complicated mess with emotionally unavailable people like Michael."

Ebony gave me a side-eye. "Not everyone is like your complicated ass fiancé? He was the worst."

I scowled. "Ex. Put some respect on that."

She raised a brow. "You sure? Wait! I don't want to know! I'm grown. No more drama."

Breaking up with Michael should've felt like a loss, like heartbreak. I felt like curling up in bed with a bottle of wine, crying over wasted years and shattered dreams.

Honestly? I felt free. Light. Like I had been carrying a burden, I didn't even realize it was weighing me down. The reality was simple—Michael had never really loved me, not in the way I needed to be loved. He loved the idea of me. I didn't ask questions. Ebony was right.

He liked how I fit into his world when convenient, but I had always been waiting. Waiting to be enough. Waiting for him to see me the way I saw him. And the truth? He never would have with his secret.

"So let me get this straight," she said, sipping her tea. She turned down another mimosa.

"You're not curled up in a ball, crying over that two-timing, non-committal, emotionally constipated liar?"

I popped a piece of bacon in my mouth. "Nope."

Her eyes narrowed. "No regrets?"

I shrugged. "None. I was tired."

She sat back, brows raised. "Damn. I'm impressed. We both have grown up. Look at God."

I smiled. "Oh wait, let me show you this."

I opened my phone and went to Michael's page. There was a photo of him and Monica. She was holding up her hand, and on it was the ring I gave him back. She was smiling, and he looked as miserable as can be.

Ebony broke the silence and said what I said when I saw it. "Damn, he moved fast."

We both laughed. I knew the reason why. I didn't tell her about his freaky side. There was no need.

"Right," I said, putting my phone down. "I wonder how she is going to get along with his mother. Then again, they both are cold-blooded. Maybe he needs a woman like his mother to keep his stupid ass in check."

Ebony laughed. "Okay, now that you're officially single, what's next?"

I sighed. "Ebony, can I breathe first?"

She held up her hands. "Of course! Of course. But, hypothetically speaking, if a certain fine-ass, smooth-voiced, and emotionally-available man was actively waiting for you to stop playing games… and running."

I rolled my eyes. "I know this is about Shawn. Let the ink on his divorce, or whatever, dry."

Ebony grinned, taking a bite of her omelet. "I don't know why you are acting brand new. That man is out here looking like a damn walking apology letter, NeeNee. He loves you. You love him. Stop being stubborn."

I exhaled, staring at my plate. "I don't know. Every time we tried, it has been some shit."

"What's to know?" she challenged. "He's is getting a divorce; it might be official. He still wants you. And you? You still want him?"

"I never said that I didn't." I shrugged.

"You didn't have to." Ebony glanced at me.

I opened my mouth to argue, but she just gave me a look. It was that look. The kind that said, bitch, don't lie to me. And the worst part? She wasn't wrong.

I hated Ebony for that. She knew me. Damn Pisces.

The truth was Shawn had never really left my mind. Not fully. Some part of me had always been waiting, even when I was pretending to move on. Waiting for what, I didn't know. Maybe for him to prove me wrong.

Or perhaps for me to finally stop running. Ebony looked at me, and then, at my phone, so I did it.

I picked up the phone to call Shawn.

Guess what?

The line was disconnected...

Tonight I Give In...

Ebony and I didn't talk about Shawn after I found out his number had changed. In all of this, I realized how selfish I had been. Maybe it was for the best.

I never once thought about Ebony. Maybe it was my turn to meddle in her life. But then something else changed things, not just for me, but for both of us.

That afternoon, Ebony's phone buzzed while we were watching a movie. She tried to ignore it. It wasn't until she picked it up for the third time that I paused the TV. Ebony got weirdly quiet. This wasn't like her.

It was just like at the bar. I frowned, "Who is that?"

Ebony hesitated, biting her lip. "So there is something I have to tell you."

I gave her a look like I spit it out.

"So I have been seeing somebody." She said

I blinked, "Okay..." I didn't take her seriously.

Ebony was dead serious this time, though. Ebony continued... "I didn't tell you because I didn't want to be all in love and annoying while you were dealing with the Michael drama."

I sat up, "Wait. What? Who?"

Ebony hesitated again. Was it a man or a woman? At this point, it wouldn't have mattered. This is Ebony.

"His name is David, and he is amazing. He is boring, but I like boring now. He likes science and books and stuff. We met at a professional development."

The way she said it—soft, uncharacteristically shy--- made me take notice. And he was a school teacher.

"Oh shit. You like this man for real."

Ebony groaned, dropping her head on the back of the couch. "I hate that I do."

"Why?" I laughed.

"Because he has me doing all of that corny shit that I used to clown you for. Smiling at my damn phone. Cancelling plans to chill with him. Cuddling, NeeNee. Me. Cuddling. Girl, I cuddle now."

I gasped dramatically, "Not you out here being somebody's little spoon."

I was still laughing when it dawned on me.

"Wait," I asked. "How long has this been going on? Ebony, I wasn't paying attention."

"Three months. Remember that night I left you at the bar, which I am glad I did. You got your back blown out. I was with him that night. Trying to beat you home. Lord knows you needed it. I really like him."

My smile faded. "Months?"

"I know," Ebony winced. "I know. I should have told you sooner. I didn't want to make it seem like I was just out here thriving while you were struggling with Michael's bullshit. Then with Shawn. I am sorry, girl."

"Ebony, that is wrong, and I apologize that you felt like that around me. That I made you feel you couldn't tell me. You are my very best friend in this world. My sister. My family. I don't care what I am going through. You could have told me. I want you to be happy." I said.

Ebony sighed and then laughed. "Girl, you know I was ready to keep things on the hush for at least another six months. I like sneaky links. I invented them."

I shook my head, laughing, "Girl, no. Now spill. Who is this man? Where does he work? Does he have good credit? How is his mother? Does he love his mother?"

Ebony grinned. "He is real solid. And funny as hell. And yes? I know what I said. He used to play basketball."

"Professionally?" I asked.

"College. Now, he teaches. He said he has this friend who just moved out here for work, and we thought of you. That's him, anxious for you to meet him."

I gave her a suspicious look. "Why?"

Ebony smirked. "Because David has been trying to hook you up with him. I told David about you. I just told him about how great you are and Michael's messy ass. Now Shawn. I want you to be happy too. "

"Oh, hell no!" I replied. "Thank you, but I am not ready for all of that. I don't need a hookup. Not now!"

Ebony pleaded. "Just meet him. No pressure. If he is ugly, fake an emergency and leave. I will understand. Damn, girl, I might leave, too. I don't do ugly."

I hesitated. Maybe it was time to open myself up again, but I thought about it. What if I wasn't ready?

Ebony looked at me, "Worst case, he is ugly. In the best case, he is nice. Either way, you are getting a free meal. Sounds like a win to me."

"How about we just have drinks," I replied.

"One," Ebony giggled as she called David...

Be Happy...

And that is how I ended up in some jazz lounge, dressed in a body-hugging dress that Ebony insisted would make any man weak in the knees. I should have stayed home. What was on TV tonight?

Not that I was trying to impress anybody. I was... just showing up. That's all. She convinced me to do more than to just have a casual drink. At least I know the guy has a job. They never said a name, though.

That was a red flag. It was waving at me.

"This is a bad idea," I said aloud.

Ebony signed dramatically. "We haven't even sat down yet. Damn, at least pretend to be open-minded. You are better than that."

I laughed because David had changed Ebony. I was just noticing that she was more congenial. Nicer. Almost, I hate to say it, giving demure? It was giving... affable. Ebony was almost too nice.

"I am open-minded." I shot her a look of concern. "Just not about blind dates set up by your man, who I have never met, but he has you whipped."

"It is not a date. It is a meeting." Ebony corrected me. "A casual dinner, maybe. Ain't nobody trying to make you fall in love over an appetizer? Lobster, maybe."

"Good," I said. "I am only here for the food. I looked at the menu online. It looks good."

Ebony laughed. "And you call me greedy."

We stepped further inside, and I must admit it was a nice place. Jazz was playing low in the background, with dim lighting and rich mahogany booths.

I saw a man, who I assumed was David was waiting at the entrance. His face lit up when he saw Ebony.

He was about five feet eleven inches tall, light-skinned, with a tall, lanky frame and sandy, light brown hair. He had an easy smile. Ebony and he would make some beautiful kids together. It made me smile.

When he saw Ebony, he pulled her into his arms and kissed her softly. I was already jealous. He radiated warmth. I loved that for him and for her.

He was dressed nicely in khakis, a nice shirt, and a nice jacket. I saw instantly that he wasn't just good to Ebony, but good for her. I smiled, thinking this is who has Ebony acting brand new. I loved it for her.

"NeeNee, this is David." Her eyes were shining.

"David, this my heart, NeeNee." She was beaming.

David nodded, gave me a handshake, and then a friendly hug. "It's nice to finally meet you. Ebony talks about you all the time."

"All good things, I hope." I smiled.

"Mostly," David teased.

Ebony swatted his arm playfully. Then, just then, as if on cue, David said he needed to make a call and excused himself. I figured he was going outside to meet his friend. My nerves were on edge.

Ebony looked at me.

"Let's go to the bar." She said, walking off.

She ordered two glasses of white wine.

I looked at Ebony and said, "I love him for you."

"Thank God," Ebony laughed. I would have lost my receipt before I tried to take him back."

The wine arrived, and I paid. I picked my glass up, and Ebony proposed a toast.

Ebony raised her glass and said, "To new beginnings, and never settling for less."

I clinked my glass against Ebony's. "I will drink to that. And this is a really nice place."

"So…" Ebony said, "While we are waiting…"

Here we go. The other shoe was about to drop. I wanted to hear this one. She could see I was nervous and was trying to break the tension.

Ebony surprised me though.

"Thank you for this," Ebony blushed.

"As much as we have been through, I am glad you finally get to be happy," I replied. I really was.

"Girl," Ebony said, "I was out here acting like our boy, Shawn, was in college with women, and had a whole roster. You remember those thirsty chicks he had."

"A what?" I laughed. And Shawn.

"A roster. A lineup. Me. I was developing a whole starting five of financially stable men. I didn't care of they were fat, tall, short, or bald. Did you see some of those girls that liked Shawn though. Looked like a zoo."

I laughed. Maybe a little too loud. I remembered.

Ebony then got serious. "I wasn't trying to fall in love, but I am. Right now, I want you to be happy for once. And if not with Shawn, somebody good. You hear me?"

"Ebony," I was ready to protest, and then, I stopped myself. I saw the concern in her eyes. I replied, "Yes."

"If this guy is not who you like, you will need somebody," Ebony said, sipping her wine. "I can't be the only one out here happy. David is a keeper."

I thought about Shawn.

I still had not heard from him.

Ebony looked at me, looking at my phone.

I realized that the idea of starting over was terrifying, as was the idea of staying in a fake relationship.

Maybe Ebony was right, and there was somebody worthy of me and me for them. First, I would have to get through to whoever Ebony's man, David, was trying to hook me up with. He might be a great guy and it was me that was looking to find fault already.

Or he was some muscle head, a former jock who would grunt all through dinner. Then again, he might be nice.

I was tripping.

Then, as if on cue again, David came back through the door, followed by the man who Ebony and I assumed was his friend. The one I was supposed to meet.

My stomach dropped as I watched David hold the door open for him. Ebony looked at me first…

Thank God, I Found You...

My mouth dropped to the floor the second I saw who it was. Was that...

Shawn. That Shawn. Shawn Shawn.

You know Shawn Jonathan Conquest!

Time slowed. The background noise faded.

It was just him. It was just us.

That same smirk.

Those auburn brown eyes.

The same full lips that used to whisper promises against my skin in college.

Time stood still.

He looked somehow better since the hotel.

Maybe even better. How?

Was it losing Keisha's dead weight?

Wait, hold on. I quickly came to my senses.

This wasn't a movie; this is real life. No more dreaming.

I whipped around to face Ebony.

"Are you kidding me?" This was too much.

Ebony held up her hands. "Oh, hell no. Before you curse me out, just listen, I didn't know shit."

I could see it in her eyes that she didn't know.

Then she said… "David, we know Shawn."

"David!" My voice was low, furious, as I spun around to look at him. "You set me up."

David looked at me and asked the only question he could as another man came through the door.

He was about five feet eight inches tall, brown-skinned, with a close haircut, and a goatee.

He saw David, walked up, and shook his hand.

He, too, looked confused at us all standing there looking at Shawn. Now I was confused.

Shawn just had that smirk.

"Who is Shawn?" David asked. "This is Jerome. This is who we were waiting for."

Jerome looked at Shawn and said, "I just walked in, and I already feel like I need to mind my business…"

Ex-Factor...

Ebony looked at David, Jerome, Shawn, and then at me and said the same thing we all were thinking. "What the fuck is going on?"

Shawn cleared his throat, stepping in. "NeeNee. Ebony. New guy number one. New guy number two. What happened? What is going on?"

I turned to Shawn, my eyes narrowing.

David was confused as can be. So was Jerome. Ebony just threw her hands up. I wanted answers.

"Wait, Ebony," David asked, "Y'all know him. I don't know him. I am so confused. He was walking in, too, so I held the door for him. Did I do something wrong?"

I was ready to say something. But what?

Ebony took over, and I thanked God.

"This is Shawn, NeeNee's... I don't know what they were. They should just get married, as messy as they are, but I love them both." She threw up her hands.

"Damn, Ebony," Shawn laughed, and then, smirked. "Is that how you feel. You gave up on me. No us?"

I looked at Shawn and asked, "What are you doing here? How did you even find us?"

He gave me that look that said whatever he was about to say was about to be the truth...

"NeeNee, I just got back in town tonight. I changed my number because of Keisha. She is crazy. You must have hurt her feelings bad that day. She destroyed my room that day at the hotel. They called the police. I was going to call you, but you know you haven't answered strange numbers since college." He was going in.

Shawn looked at Jerome. "So, I said I would text you once I got settled. I just moved right down the street. I had no clue you were even here. I was just hungry and saw this place earlier. And so… we good?"

"That is true," I heard Ebony mumble behind me. "Used to eat up all of our food, and still all muscle, all through college. But I told you, NeeNee, he might be psychic when it comes to you. He will find your ass. Just look."

That's when it clicked for David and all of us. David looked at Shawn. "So you didn't know they were here. You walked in with me; they thought you were my friend, and I was setting you up with NeeNee. My bad, bro. I apologize for the confusion, NeeNee."

Shawn looked at me, but said to David, "You're good bro. It's my bad. She is worth it though. By the way, I am Shawn Conquest. Nice to meet you."

David laughed. "David. This is Jerome."

Shawn then looked at Jerome. "My bad, bro, for holding you up. What is this? Is this a first date or a hostage situation? You look nervous, bro. But, take good care of her. If she says she is over me, that is her telling you, not herself. If you need a survival guide, I got notes."

David and Jerome laughed at that. He's not funny.

I felt dumb. I just accused Shawn of stalking me, and this was purely coincidental. Who knew that he would change his number from Keisha? I didn't.

Ebony shifted her eyes between me and Shawn. "Oh shit, girl. Looks like fate to me."

David looked at Ebony, and then, at Shawn, "My bad for drawing you into that, Shawn! NeeNee, I apologize."

Shawn looked at David, "No problem. She broke my heart, but I am good now. I cried. David? And you must be with Ebony. And you picked her with both eyes open? Damn. Bless your heart, you must really like a challenge. I am glad she stopped biting people."

David laughed, and Ebony swatted David's arm. Here Shawn was cracking jokes, as usual.

Ebony feigned outrage, "That was one time, and he deserved it. But, I still got hands."

Shawn hugged Ebony tightly. This time, she didn't push him away. Jerome was still stuck.

Shawn, now serious, replied, "No. But I will let you get back to your date." He looked at Jerome, "Bro Bro, you look like you read directions on a box. If she starts looking at her phone, she isn't feeling you. But if she does, take care of her for me. I still love her!"

Ebony mumbled. "In a city of millions of people. He walked into this juke joint. Damn, NeeNee."

Shawn never stopped staring at me. He stuck his hands in his pocket, which I finally realized was a sign that he was hiding his feelings after all of these years. I exhaled sharply, looking back at Shawn.

And the way he was looking at me? He gave me that same mischievous smile as if he had been waiting for this moment. It did something to me. Something dangerous. Something I wasn't ready for.

So I did what I did best. I was ready to run. I looked at Jerome, who was still stuck, and said only I could...

"I am sorry." To nobody in particular, and everybody.

My eyes shifted between Ebony and David. Ebony looked at me, almost pleading for me not to do it. She looked at Shawn, but I turned and walked away.

I think it was because I was more so embarrassed that I was ready to give up on Shawn over a phone number. Not even another woman's, but because he had a valid reason why he changed his number. I felt stupid.

It was always something. And I upset Keisha that bad?

And after all of these years, I realized who it was that has hurt me the most. I knew that there are only three people that could truly hurt you, if you allowed them to, your friends, your family, and yourself. This was all me.

This time though, I ran as fast as my legs could carry me. Ebony must have said something to him, or maybe he was tired of me just leaving, maybe a combination of both, because this time, Shawn didn't let me go...

I Call Your Name…

I burst out of the building, my breath ragged, my heart was slamming against my ribs, like it was trying to break free from my chest.

The warm night air was thick and suffocating, doing nothing to cool the fire burning under my skin. This was too much, entirely too much.

My vision blurred, not from the night air, but from the weight pressing down on me.

I needed air. I needed space.

I needed to be anywhere but here.

But before I could get too far, his hand found me. I had gotten only half of a block away before he stopped me.

Warm. Familiar. Unshakable.

"NeeNee, so, again, you are really not going to talk to me at all. Just like that. You know you are the first woman that ever broke up with me, and we weren't even together. I should be mad! What did I do?"

That voice. That damn voice. And he got jokes.

I froze. Why was I running anyway?

"What do you want me to say," I asked. "What do you want me to do, Shawn. I don't know how to do this."

"I want you to stop running." He was serious. "I told you what happened, and this is what you do?"

It wasn't a command. It wasn't a plea. It was something else entirely—something raw, something broken. Something that made my chest tighten until I could barely breathe. I squeezed my eyes shut.

Don't turn around.

Don't let him do this to you.

Don't let him pull you back in.

"Shawn, I am confused." But this was fate. He was here. "Why can't we get this right?

"I don't know." His grip tightened just enough to make me feel it—to ensure that I knew he meant every word. "What I do know is what it's like to lose you. I can't do that again. And over a phone number. Not Keisha."

I swallowed hard, keeping my back to him.

"Shawn, but…." My voice cracked, betraying me. "Right now, I feel dumb. Stupid. Don't…"

"Don't what?" He let out a sharp breath. "Don't fight for you? Don't tell you I was a fool? How I should've come after you the second you walked away? How many times? It is hard to breathe without you, NeeNee. I tried. I came back here for you. I moved here for us!"

His voice wavered just a little. Still, it hit like a wrecking ball, shattering every wall I tried to build between us. I felt every single word. His words did that to me.

"I had a choice back then," he said, voice thick with regret. "And I chose wrong. I told myself that if you wanted to go, that I wasn't enough to make you stay. But I was wrong, NeeNee. You are the only one who ever knew me or tried to get to know me. Ever."

"Hear me out. I should've fought for you. I should've made you see that no matter what we went through or how messy it got… It was always you and me? We were supposed to find our way back to each other."

I closed my eyes. "Like now?"

"Yes." His voice was desperate now. "NeeNee, please. —look at me. I can't keep letting you walk away from me. Think about how many times I have. And the only thing my dumb ass can do is watch you leave. Look at me. I want you to see me. Look at me."

I did. And damn it, I shouldn't have.

Because his eyes… They swallowed me whole. They always did since the day we met.

"I got nothing left, NeeNee. I'm a grown man, but I have nowhere else to go. My marriage failed—not because of you, but because it was never real."

I could see he was crying. "I let my whole life fall apart because I couldn't get over you. Until there was nothing left of me but memories of you and me. There is no one else for me. And I don't care about any of that. All I care about is right now. What I feel at this moment."

He stepped closer, his voice breaking. "And right now, I'm standing here, Nee, begging you—don't leave me. Don't walk away. I can't do this without you, with me."

My chest ached. My heart twisted, tangled in everything I thought I buried.

"You don't understand," I whispered.

"Yes, I do," he said through gritted teeth. "I understand everything. Why you left? Why you never looked back? Why you're scared even right now? If taking the blame means you'll stop pushing me away, I'll take it. It will risk anything and everything for us again."

His voice dropped to a whisper. "NeeNee, I will take the hurt. The guilt. The regret. I'll carry all of it if you'll let yourself love me again. There is so much I should have said; I could have said. But we are here now."

A tear slipped down my cheek. He was here.

"Every time I close my eyes, it's you," he said, voice shaking. "I can't do this without you."

"Every time I think about what love is—what it's supposed to feel like—it's you. And I don't know how to exist in a world where you don't love me back." He was crying now. "What else do I have to say. I am stumbling. My pain keeps getting in the way."

I bit my lip hard, trying to keep it together.

"Tell me what we had meant nothing," he pushed. "Tell me you don't remember how we laughed until we cried. Tell me you don't remember the way you used to curl

266

up in my arms like it was the only place you ever felt safe. Please tell me that, and I will walk away."

He swallowed hard. "Say it, baby, and I'll let you go. I am used to you running away from me now, but I told you, whenever you are ready to stop running, I will be right here. I am still here. I have always been here. So say it. Tell me what to say to make you stay."

I opened my mouth and closed it.

Nothing came out because I remembered.

I remembered the way he kissed me like I was his whole world. That's because I was. The way his voice softened when he whispered my name. The way his arms always felt like home. What his lips felt like both then and now. Was that enough though?

"You once told me you don't believe anything is meant to be," Shawn said. "But I do, and if you stand here and tell me you don't feel this, I'll let you go one last time. Go ahead, NeeNee. I dare you. I dare you."

His voice cracked. His pain was reaching for me, pulling me under. Then he said, in almost a whisper. "I have nowhere else to go, NeeNee. Not without you."

"Because no matter where I run, it always comes back to you. Look at us right now. My God, if I knew you would call me, I wouldn't have changed my number, but Keisha, she wouldn't let up after she saw you. Baby listen. Stop running. I'm here now. I told you." He said.

267

I looked at him, and I remembered the first time he fell asleep in my room. I loved how safe he made me feel, and I wanted that feeling again.

He took a step forward and looked at me.

"I'm right here. Stop running…" he said.

And he stepped closer to me, and I stepped back. I saw a look of fear cross his face.

And I closed my eyes, wondering if this was even real. I opened them, and he was still right there.

Shawn stepped closer to me and said, "Talk to me."

Then I spoke…

On Bended Knee...

So I wasn't dreaming. Shawn was really right here, in New York. I was single, and he was divorced.

I took a step back from him, took a deep breath, and said what I should have said the last time.

"If I could go back," I said, my voice raspy. "I wish to God that I never met you, Shawn Conquest."

Shawn tried to speak, but he said enough.

"Just shut up, Shawn." I started again. My voice was firm. I saw the hurt register on his face, but he said what he needed to say, and now, it was my turn.

"I wish you never spoke to me that day in class. I wish I never answered your text. I wish we never kissed. That I never made love to you that night in my dorm. Then I wouldn't be standing here now. Needing you."

I continued, voice shaking, "I wouldn't have to live with this regret that I let you walk away. I wouldn't have to stand here and see you looking at me like I'm the one who broke you. So no, I won't say it. I still love you."

My lips trembled. "I think I have been in love with you since the first day I met you. I just thought that my love wasn't enough for you. That I wasn't good enough for you. I didn't didn't have anything back then to give you but my love. That broken, little girl from Philly."

"I thought it wasn't enough because you chose Keisha over me. I wanted you to be happy. I thought she could make you happy. But I still wanted you. Being so naïve

269

and immature, I still wanted you like a kid wants a toy on Christmas morning. And just as fast, I broke you."

Shawn's jaw clenched, but he didn't move.

"But I never forgot you," I whispered. "I still needed you every day since the day I met you. I told myself that if I wasn't strong enough to love you, I had to be strong enough to let you go. And when you walked away without putting up a fight, I thought I made the right decision. I let you walk away."

Silence stretched between us, heavy with everything we couldn't still say.

My heart pounded. My body screamed to run—to do what I always did best. But my feet wouldn't move.

Shawn didn't move.

He looked at me and said something, I wasn't expecting. He asked, "Are you done?"

"Done what?" I asked confused.

"Running and talking?" Shawn reached for my hand.

Shawn stepped closer and there was that smirk. "If I mean anything to you, pay attention to the fact that even though you said all of that, I'm still here. "

His voice was barely above a whisper, but it slammed into me like a freight train, and I still heard every word. "Don't act like I don't still see you. Like I don't still love you. How much time we wasted. I needed you too."

My throat tightened. "You don't know me anymore. The party is over. I am a mess. Look at me."

He laughed bitterly, moving closer, and pressing his forehead to mine. "Then teach me. Let me stay after the party is over and be the one to help you clean up."

My tears blurred my vision.

"You might not like me. Or like what you see."

He smiled, "Let me decide, and until you are strong enough, I will love you for both of us. God kept sending you to me for a reason. Look at us now."

"You don't want me," I tried to laugh. "You want who I used to be. I'm not her anymore. I have changed."

"That's bullshit." His voice was authentic. "And you know it. As long as your name is NeeNee, I want you, and that means the good and the bad. Any mistakes we make is why God made erasers. This is not just for people who make mistakes, but also for the people who want to fix them. Give me that chance. Try for me."

He ran a hand over his face, exhaling sharply. "You think I wanted to do this? You think I wanted to chase you down, to practically beg you to see me every time? You know I will always be the one thing you can't lie to yourself, or God, about. You love me."

"I do love you," I confessed. "I always have."

"Yeah," Shawn smiled. "That's what I thought. I love you too. I always have and always will."

"Stop running, NeeNee," he pleaded, voice breaking. "I'm here. I have nowhere else to go." He swallowed hard. "You don't get to decide this for both of us. Not anymore. I don't need perfection. I just always needed you. We are not trying anymore. We are doing this."

"But what if...' I replied.

"What did I say?" Shawn said it in a way that let me know that he meant it. "We aren't trying anymore. We are doing. We are doing this. Me and you. You run again; we aren't going back. We stay and fix this."

I realized what my first mistake had been in life. When it comes to past pain and trauma, some people work through that pain, and some people become it.

And just like that...I did what I should have done years ago. I stopped running... finally!

And Shawn?

Shawn was right here as he had promised.

Right here.

Waiting.

For me.

All I Want Is Forever…

Maybe I was tired. Tired of fighting. Tired of running.

Tired of pretending that I didn't love him anymore with every broken piece of my heart.

I couldn't fight it anymore.

I hated the way he made me feel.

I hated the way he made me want to stay.

I forced myself to look at him, really look at him. He was a storm that I had never been able to outrun.

It didn't matter. I was where I needed to be.

I was searching his face for something, anything, to give me a reason to fight how I felt and what I was feeling. I couldn't find one single thing.

He was my missing puzzle piece.

I could breathe now.

I didn't want to run.

So I let him kiss me.

Shawn pulled back… "I'm not letting you go this time."

I didn't have anywhere else to go…

Whatever It Takes…

The kiss was instant. Desperate, years of want and regret tangles in the way our lips met, in the way his hands slid into my hair, in the way I pressed against him like I was trying to crawl inside of his skin.

And when his lips met mine, every emotion I had buried came crashing down. Regret. Longing. Love.

I let him pull me closer, let his hands roam my body like he was memorizing me all over again for his future benefit. And when he whispered, "Come with me," I knew there was no turning back.

We barely made it inside his apartment before our clothes started coming off.

It wasn't rushed. It wasn't frantic.

It was slow. Intense.

Like we were both relearning each other. His hands, lips, and body were all too much and still not enough.

I don't know.

And when he finally pushed inside me, both of us gasping at the contact, I knew—he knew. I was home.

I lay there after we were done and stared at the ceiling.

I heard Shawn speak first.

"I am afraid to close my eyes." He mused.

I looked at him, confused. "Why?"

He replied, "I am scared if I do, I will wake up, and this will all be a dream. I know this is crazy right now, and we have a lot to figure out, but tell me you won't leave again. Please. Promise me that. Loving you is not an option to me. It is what I need right now."

I moved next to him. And didn't say another word at first. There was nothing else that needed to be said. Then, I realized why I used to hate myself.

I was angry at myself for not being strong enough to deal with the things I went through when I was younger. It was true. I was always apologizing for when they fucked up. My mother. My father. Shirley. Michael.

I know now that I was stronger than I thought if it allowed me to become who I am.

I had to learn to be still. To be quiet.

I often wondered how the devil knew how to bring certain chaos into my life. I told him. I spoke my fears out loud and he brought them. Basically, I taught him.

I never asked God for what I wanted, like this. When I did. When I finally did, he sent Shawn. Shawn Shawn.

So I looked at Shawn and said, "I won't. I'm tired of running from you and me. And, like you, I don't have anywhere else to go. I promise. And if I do go anywhere, it will be with you."

Shawn looked at me, "I promise the same with you..."

After The Love Has Lost Its Shine...

The morning light filtered through the windows, casting a warm glow on Shawn's bedroom.

I stirred, stretching slightly before I realized I wasn't alone. That this wasn't a dream. He was really here.

Shawn. Say it with me. Shawn Jonathan Conquest. That Shawn. Shawn Shawn. His arm was draped across my waist, his breathing slow and steady.

Last night had been everything. Passionate. Intense. Unforgiving in its honesty. One of those nights where morning came too soon. Now that the high was wearing off, the reality was creeping back in. This was us now.

I turned carefully, watching him sleep. His face was peaceful, as if he needed that rest.

There was something else. There was something in his expression that made my heart flutter.

Something reassuring.

For the first time in years, he looked whole again, as if he was finally where he belonged. He looked peaceful.

He was happy. More importantly, I was happy.

I let my fingers trail across his jaw before I could stop myself. Shawn's eyes fluttered open, his gaze was warm as his eyes locked onto mine.

He smiled at me, and I smiled back.

"Morning," he murmured. His voice was husky with sleep. His breath still didn't stink. I laughed.

I replied, as I laid back down, "Good morning."

Shawn sat up, kissed me, and then, he softly kissed my shoulder. "So what happens now? You know we didn't eat at all yesterday. I'm starving."

I laughed. "We stay together. And we can eat."

"And let me make this all easy." He turned me towards him, his eyes soft. "Will you marry me?"

I blinked, my heart stopping. "Shawn—"

"I am in love with you, NeeNee," he whispered, brushing the hair from my face. "Just marry me."

My throat went dry. "This is crazy. I am in love with you, too. Ebony is about to have a field day. Yes, I will."

"Good," he laughed. He kissed my forehead. "But this right here is real. No more running. You are safe now. I got you. Besides, my knees are bad now. My back. Oh no, my back. You know I got these bad ankles."

I laughed. "You play entirely too much.

Everything had changed, and yet, it didn't. Shawn was still Shawn. He was still so silly. I loved it.

"Yes, I will marry you." I said, then I kissed him.

Shawn looked at me and said, "Wait until my Mom and Dad meet you. I told them about you—about us. My

Pop was on me, like, stop playing, boy. My Mom is going to love you. She says I finally got somebody to ground me. Wait until they find out you tried to dump me over a phone number. You have no shame."

I laughed, "You told them about me?"

Shawn looked at me like I said something crazy. "When I first met you. I wanted you to meet them that day. They wanted to thank you for helping me. Then, I told them how I saw you again. My Mom claimed she knew back then. That lady plays too much. She claims she was letting me make up my mind after the stuff with Keisha. Max said I was a dummy to let you go."

Before I could respond, my phone buzzed on the nightstand. It was a text from Ebony.

From Ebony: Blink twice if y'all did it. I know you did.

I now owe Ms. Anita Baker an apology for saying what I said about fairytales. I was listening to the wrong song. I should have been listening to "Giving You The Best That I Got," "Just Because," or "Plenty Of Room."

And then, I looked at Shawn, who was laughing his head off. He wouldn't stop.

"What," I asked curiously. Did he see the text?

Shawn laughed again. "You left the guy, Jerome, at the restaurant. Sipping on melted ice. Had the band dedicating songs to his broken heart. He got left on read in real life. I bet old boy is mad as fuck..."

I Have Nothing...

After years of heartbreak, hard choices, and lessons that nearly broke me, I finally learned the one thing no one bothered to teach me. Love should never cost me my peace. It shouldn't cost you yours either.

And that sometimes, life hurts. People will hurt you. This one thing that most people miss though is that even if the wound, or what hurt you was not your fault, the healing is most certainly your responsibility.

In my relationship with Michael, I spent too many years fighting for him, and it wasn't worth the battle. Look how that turned out. He used me as a smoke screen to mask his—stuff. Lord, sweet Jesus.

Shawn. He has always been different.

He loved without condition, without cages, without a need to break me to keep me. He saw my every scar and wound that I thought would never heal, and he kissed them like they were beautiful. He stayed.

He was really here. More importantly, I was here.

Our bond didn't happen overnight. Like all real love, we took our time. I finally stopped running and let myself believe I deserved something good. I met Shawn at the beginning of forever. We built something from ashes. Something honest. Something unshakeable.

We got married in Atlanta. It wasn't anything big. Just Ebony's grandmother, Ms. Mary, her man, Mr. Monroe, Ebony and David, me and Shawn, Shawn's parents,

Carolyn and John, who people call Mr. Johnny, Shawn's brother, Max, and his girlfriend, Yolanda.

Shawn's family had his grandparents, uncles, aunts, cousins, and close family friends. We even invited Jerome and some girl named April that he met that night I left him. I know, right. I felt bad. We're good now. Ebony was my maid of honor and Shawn's childhood best friend, Montana served as his best man.

No, I didn't invite anybody else. I didn't need to. They didn't deserve to enjoy this moment. What did they give me? This wasn't about them. Our joy and happiness didn't need an audience. Just us, lots of music, and good food. Even Keisha couldn't ruin this day.

And when I looked into Shawn's eyes, he was happy. We danced barefoot in the middle of our hotel room that first night and were happy to my favorite song, "If I Were A Bell" by Teena Marie. I love me some Teena. For once, I introduced Shawn to a song, and not the other way around with him. He loved it.

And, of course, we danced to Shawn's favorite song, "I Have Nothing," by Whitney Houston. Shawn finally explained the words, and said it reminded him of me. And Shawn kept his promise. He was here. Our love was simple. It didn't hurt. It didn't take. It didn't leave.

Did I tell you? I am pregnant! I know right.

Don't worry. The baby is doing fine. But Shawn won't let us leave his sight. It is a boy that we are naming him "Shawnior." Oh, so you were paying attention…. Good!

Epilogue:

We were in the middle of game night, and Shawn and I had been whipping David and Ebony's ass in spades when our food arrived. Jerome and April had just arrived, too. It was our couples' night.

I put on some music and looked at Shawn as he grabbed plates for the Chinese takeout food that we had just ordered. Did I tell you that I can't cook?

Our baby is due in three months. We were all excited.

The minute Babyface's voice came on, Shawn looked at me and smiled. Ebony laughed, and promised to tell David why it was our wedding dance song.

Just then, the music on my phone stopped, when I was ready to put it down. It began to ring with an unfamiliar 215 number, shattering the moment as the caller ID told another story. Area code 215 is in Pennsylvania.

It said, "Reginald Willams."

My father... Reggie.

Or whatever they called him. That Reggie.

The past came calling, and I decided to answer it.

The man who had built a whole new life without me and my mother. Why was he calling me? Why now?

His story was so messy that I didn't have time to explain it. Nor would I even try. It is that deep.

The man who never once tried to reach out was calling.

The man who never once tried to fix what he broke.

I frowned as I answered it. "Hello?"

"Nicole?" It was a woman's voice.

The voice on the other end was hesitant. Familiar.

"This is Loretta. Your father's wife."

It felt like the air was knocked out of my lungs.

"Nicole," she said to make sure I was still there.

This bitch.

"It's NeeNee! Not Nicole or Nikki. What do you want?"

Her conversation would never be long enough or strong enough to make me like her. I am grown.

I saw Ebony staring at me.

"Okay, NeeNee. It's about your father..."

"What about him? And why now?" I asked.

Wait, how did she get my number to even call me from his phone? Every muscle in my body went stiff.

Shawn stopped and looked at me, with concern etched across his face. Shawn touched my arm gently. I put it on speaker. I had nothing to hide, Shawn knew.

"He was in an accident today," she replied. "And he's asking for you... He wants to see you."

I may have picked the wrong time to stop running.

My past had found me. "I will call when I can come."

And I hung up. Was I ready deal with this?

The only difference, as I looked at my husband, Shawn, was that I knew I had somebody there who would help me deal with all of it. I looked at Shawn, who was standing there. He leaned over and kissed me.

"I need to go home." I said to him, and the others.

Shawn looked at me, his eyes full of questions... "To Philly? We'll go after we eat. I got you. I got us."

He instinctively touched my back and my stomach.

He became our protector, and those moves showed it.

I looked at him and smiled. "I know. Thank you."

Yeah, I was tired of running. It was time, and I had questions. Ones only my father could answer. I wanted to know what really happened with and to my mother. Maybe he knew where she went. Maybe he didn't.

As Babyface's voice began to sing again, I sat down to eat, not for my sake, but for my baby.

And I apologize to you. I haven't told you everything. It wasn't deliberate. You went through all of this and I never told you my full name. Or my parents' names.

Let me reintroduce myself... It is Nicole Williams.

My name is Nicole Williams Conquest now. I am Renee and Reggie's daughter. That Reggie and Renee. As in "Ree-Nay." Don't ever call me Nay Nay. Only NeeNee. Like Dee Dee. CeCe. BeBe. It is only part of my story.

I wear my name like a string of diamonds around my neck now. It's the first and last thing that I will ever own in my life. You should too. Correct people about it.

Never be ashamed of yours. I am not.

And your story... The story you have, that might have nearly cost your life, will inspire others to live their lives to the fullest. And sometimes you will be tested, not to show your weakness, but to discover your strength.

My parents. You might have heard about them years ago... and why they split up. It was never about me. It was something deeper and more complicated than me.

There is that word again. What they did wasn't right. Now you know why I never wanted to be like them. Especially after my mother... never mind. I think Michael's mother knew. Had she checked me out?

According to Shirley, their real drama started when my mother found out she was a side chick, and my mother, being messy, introduced me to his girlfriend. Her name was Nicole, but everybody called her Nikki. She is who my father named me after. How? Why, I don't know...

Find out how NeeNee's story really began in…

**Author Rasheed Clark's Explosive Debut Novel:
"Stories I Wouldn't Tell Nobody But God…"**

Not since Terry McMillan's "Waiting To Exhale," has a book been so raw, gritty and honest about love, loss, family, relationships, acceptance and trust and put a voice to the collective frustration felt by millions of people looking for love in all of the wrong places.

Finally, somebody will tell the truth about the lies that we tell ourselves.

"Stories I Wouldn't Tell Nobody But God," the long awaited, explosive debut novel by Rasheed Clark, is an emotionally charged, provocative and page-turning story of four friends: Sista, Brian, Day, and Nikki and the rollercoaster ride that they call their lives, through triumph and tragedy…

…Sista, who will lose the only man that she has ever truly loved, as she allows her weight to determine her self-worth.

…Brian, who must learn the hard way that a good woman isn't hard to find, he just has to be man enough to keep her.

…Day, who must learn to accept himself for who, and what he is.

…Nikki, whose perfect world is shattered when she chooses to love a man more than she has ever loved herself, and it almost, cost her, her life, because of that man's infidelity and lies.

Powerfully told, heartwarming and funny, "Stories I Wouldn't Tell Nobody But God" will leave you wanting more.

There are many things, stories that many people wouldn't tell nobody but God, and still so much more that many people tend to keep to themselves, out of fear that nobody but God would understand…until now.

And now, read an excerpt of Nikki's story that started it all… and discover for yourself how NeeNee got her real name: Nicole and from who…

Nikki...

Wait, this can't be happening,' I thought to myself. I looked at the girl, then at the little girl and instantly, I knew. Renee, that's the name she gave me, attempted to snap me out of my daze as I stared at her daughter.

I regained my composure and looked at Renee again.

'And you are?'

'Renee,' Renee said suddenly confused but then she realized that I didn't know her. 'I am Reggie's daughter's mother.'

'Reggie?' I said. This felt like some soap opera shit.

'Reggie,' Renee said again. 'Tall, dark-skinned and he got a bald head. This is our daughter, Nicole.' I could see that.

'He'll be here soon. He called from the airport. Would you like to come in?' I said moving aside. But she didn't move.

She just looked at me. I just looked at her, finally realizing that I just met my man's daughter's mother for the first time, a child that I never knew about to begin with.

I wasn't hurt though, I wanted answers.

"Listen, I think we really need to talk.'

'Talk? About what?' Renee said eyeing me suspiciously. 'We don't need to talk about nothing. Who are you?' This chick is ghetto.

'Wait a minute,' I said taking a minute to check myself. I was through with being polite. So I leaned in so that her daughter didn't hear.

'I see you need the remix. You slept with my man and you are coming off like you are the injured party. Let's try this again, bitch. I said we need to talk.'

'Can we talk woman to woman? Are you at least woman enough to do that? Or should I skip the preliminaries and just beat your natural black ass?'

Renee looked hesitantly at me again then at her daughter. I guess she thought about it for a second and realized I was serious.

So Renee walked in, holding Nicole's hand tight, as I moved aside. I took a deep breath and closed the door. It was on and I wouldn't have it any other way...

Finish Nikki's explosive story of infidelity, lies and betrayal in Rasheed Clark's long awaited 'Stories I Wouldn't Tell Nobody But God' and discover for yourself what has been keeping thousands readers up at night. This is the one book you won't be able to put down and won't soon forget...

Then... discover for yourself what kind of dirty secrets would drive a woman to commit murder in the shocking sequel to "Stories I Wouldn't Tell Nobody But God..." Rasheed Clark's "Cold Summer Afternoon."

From Author Rasheed Clark, here is a preview of the shocking sequel... "Cold Summer Afternoon."

Love. Infidelity. Deception. Abuse. Lies. Shameful secrets. Hurt. Mistrust.

For one of four women, it's enough to drive her to commit murder...

April... Trapped in a loveless marriage to a less than loving, abusive husband, she was alone until she meets Brian Robinson, who just lost the love of his life. Will she risk her marriage and make the ultimate sacrifice to find love again?

Renee... She made the transition from being the "other woman" to being one man's wife, but at what cost? She soon discovers what goes around truly does come around.

Blue... She must discover the hard way that you can't run from your past or yourself, especially when a man is involved? What will she do when she comes face to face with the man she promised to love forever?

Loretta...After destroying her own marriage through her own lies, infidelity and insecurities, she now holds the fate of another marriage in her hands. Wait until the man's wife finds out...

Brace yourself for a story you won't soon forget. Filled with more twists and turns than a rollercoaster, Cold Summer Afternoon is the book everybody will be talking about right up to its surprising ending... and **here is an excerpt, just for you! Take a peak!**

An Angry Woman Says…

I sat in the dark of my apartment for over an hour. The only light came from the street lamp outside my apartment building.

I looked around trying to figure out the number of times I wanted to burn this place down to the ground just like Left Eye tried to do to Andre Rison's place. Okay, maybe that was an accident. I was just that upset.

I thought about the times I wanted to poison his food and watch him gasp for his last breath. I would then just finish my untouched dinner and then plan his funeral. I wanted him to suffer as much as possible.

Then, I'd be happy. Maybe.

I picked up my drink and swirled the ice around in the glass and then ran my hand across the gun. It was lying on the cushion of the couch next to me. I wanted to make sure it was still there. It felt cool to my touch.

Touching it, I thought about all of the arguments, the fights, the lies and the threats that came down to this one moment. I wanted him to die. In my mind, I already died several times inside. I wanted him to hurt just as much as I do now.

For far too long, I put up with his brand of drama like some people put up with a headache. The only difference is that now payback is a bitch.

I didn't plan on killing him at first, but right now, I didn't have the strength to live with what he has done. At least what he did to me, I didn't even want to think about it. My blood ran cold when I did.

Now, sitting here, I realized he could take everything from me. I realized that my happily ever after fairytale was all built on a lie. I looked around again and had to ask myself what would drive a woman to murder?

How did I let it get to this point? I should have left. I should have been strong enough to walk away. It doesn't matter.

I know how I planned to end it.

I am going to finish it my way. I put my drink down on the coffee table and ran my hand across the gun again. It was still there.

Where was he?

I took a deep breath and waited. Hold on. Wait. You hear that? I heard the familiar jingle of the keys to the front door. He's home.

I picked up the gun, stood up and aimed it at the door. I wasn't sure if he would turn on the lights. I prayed he wouldn't. My hands started to shake.

I felt my palms grow damp under the weight of the gun. There were six bullets in the gun and every one of them belonged to him.

Slowly, the door opened. I heard a voice. Then, a brighter light washed over the room overtaking the light from the street lights outside.

I closed my eyes and pulled the trigger. Boom. Boom. Boom. Boom. Boom. Five shots. I didn't want to open my eyes until the gun was empty and hopefully, he was dead…

So after you have read, "Stories I Wouldn't Tell Nobody But God," finish the story, and find out what kind of secrets would drive a woman to commit murder in Rasheed Clark's "Cold Summer Afternoon."

Buy your copies wherever quality books are sold. You will want to read these books again!

About The Author...

I hate talking about myself. I am boring, in my mind, despite having been to places like Gettysburg and Salem, Massachusetts, the witch city. I am a different person to many different people. I even have an Italian Wikipedia page somebody created.

I asked Alexa, "Who is Author Rasheed Clark?" I got an answer. To me, I am just Rasheed Clark. Some people, I inspire; others, I intimidate. Nobody would believe I lost my mother when I was 17 and still became the man she raised me to be. My Mom and my brother were only 34 when I lost them. I move like a team; however, this has been all me. A one-man show.

I think I am supposed to say that Rasheed Clark was born in Philadelphia, Pennsylvania. However, this would start to sound like a funeral program instead of giving off the energy of the main character.

I could talk about my education... how I earned an associate's degree in business administration at Peirce College. I earned a bachelor's degree in finance and a minor in management from the former Philadelphia College of Textile and Science, which became Philadelphia University, before merging to become part of Thomas Jefferson University. Crazy stuff.

There I earned the Faculty Scholarship for Academic Excellence, and was on Peirce's Dean's List for two straight years. I didn't just go to college; I graduated. Why does it matter? I used to be the only Black person sitting in my class on any given day. Let me be great!

Then, there is the school that was so nice that I went there twice... the Drexel University. Not bad for somebody who failed every last class, except world history in the ninth grade at the Parkway Program, a magnet high school, because I was bored and I hated school. I know, and still became a teacher.

My Mom said the teachers had theirs, and to go get mine. It wasn't until after she passed that I realized that she meant getting a quality education, so I did just that.

I fell in love with the Drexel campus in the sixth grade when I was placed in a mentally gifted program for seventh and eighth graders. My class went there for ten weeks for a unique program. There, I earned my Master's degree in education, and later, my Master's degree in Education Administration and my principal certification (kindergarten through 12th grade.)

When I graduated, my friend Ethel asked me to look to my left and right. I was the only Black man, or Black person, earning a Master's degree in education that year. It was 2004, and the Drexel University. I was accepted into the University of Pennsylvania in 1996, but chose Textiles and Science. For graduate school, there was only one choice: Drexel University.

I was honored in 2006 with the Walmart Teacher of Year after being nominated by one of my former students, Jennifer, who wrote, as she said, on "the (form's) front and back" about me. This young lady would write anyone, even the president.

I came back that year after surviving a near-fatal car accident to take over her class that had not had a teacher in two months. So, you see my work ethic.

In 2008, I was honored with an Urban Education Leadership Award after my former students spoke highly of me. I would later receive an invitation to an event held by our former first lady, Michelle Obama.

I was also honored by the then-Governor of Pennsylvania, Edward Rendell, and both houses of the Pennsylvania state legislature for my other efforts.

Very few people believed in my vision for life, and not many would listen outside of my mother. At one point, I dropped out of high school, but then, God intervened. I got a call from a childhood friend named Neil, who called to tell me about the birth of his son.

He asked how I was doing, and about school. I told him I stopped going. That I dropped out. He was the only one who said what I needed to hear. Something that I carried with me for years and repeated often in my classroom. That it is not "when you start, but as long as you finish." I went back, and I graduated with honors.

I was honored with the "PNC Bank Pride In Performance Award," given to one student in an area high school who overcame incredible odds to still graduate high school and one of the most improved students in the district awards. I went from three F's, two D's, and a B to 3 A's, two B's, and two C's.

Back when no one cared that I just lost my mother. Mental health for a Black young man wasn't a topic.

I thank Neil for that. See, I listen. You just have to talk to me nicely. That's why it's always important what you say to people and how, especially your children. Your words often become their conscience when you are not around. My mother's words are still my moral compass. I thank God for my mother and her words of wisdom.

The one thing I never do now is doubt myself. My life is proof of that and the fact that God is good. He kept me. I pray that you don't doubt yourself either. Sometimes, as they say, our thoughts are backed up by so many insecurities that they create the lies that we tend to believe about ourselves. Lies to help us sleep at night.

Lauryn Hill once said, "See fantasy is what people want, but reality is what they need. I retired from the fantasy part." That is how I feel about my life.

And it is not bragging if you actually did it. I did these things. Saying what you can't do means saying what you won't do. People like that still want the rewards and bragging rights. Then, they hate you because they can't get it. They never put in the work to obtain it.

To me, jealousy is a lazy form of love. Jealousy and envy are already weak emotions. People would rather hate you, than find greatness within themselves.

By the way, my first two books garnered an impressive 15 Infinity Award nominations. This is my ninth book. Every book that I wrote did still sells, so there isn't much I can say about that. The titles, I won't tell. You could have bought it and never knew it was me.

Over the years, I have used the power of my pen to fight public corruption, mismanagement, and waste and to support the world around me. My sole goal in life, after the life I have lived, is to one day close my eyes and not have a single regret. I still don't.

I am living life, not allowing life to live me. You cannot do both. I hope you do, too. And I live a very quiet life now. I am already Rasheed Clark. Trust me, I am great.

A man. A father. Brother. Son. Grandson. Uncle. Great-Uncle. Cousin. Nephew. Friend. Great-grandson. Educator. Mentor. Pop Pop. Poppa Clark. A student. Post-graduate level educated. I've been him.

If somebody wanted me to be any different, somehow better, they would have shown me how. I am who I am—the man that God created me to be, the man that my mother raised me to be, and built her team around to get me to this point. There is no future in fronting.

She said nothing should stop me from being the man I was meant to be from sun up to sun down. I am here. I am out here, making my mother and everyone who helped raise me proud. Everyone is my teacher, even if it is to teach me what not to be. So, stand down.

And as always, proceeds from my book sales have gone towards everything from sponsoring student trips, as a teacher, to supporting battered women, breast cancer research and services, heart disease research, the Special Olympics, and my favorite: food banks that help feed thousands of people daily and so much more, and still will. You helped me do that by buying a book!

With this book, for all of the real NeeNees and Shawns, my eye is on colleges and universities. How can I help them? I was that broke college kid once, and I still live that way to this day. I will figure it out.

Until then, thank you again.